Prologue
England 1631

    Dixce looked at the blue sky then the water; they were almost the same color this morning as he viewed them from the bow of the four-masted galleon. Winter had finally ended allowing the ice on the river to melt and spring was here. The cool breeze caressed his face and blew his brown hair off his forehead. The smell of salt water was strong as the tide rose in the river and overpowered the stink of rotting fish. Seagulls swooped and shrieked as they fought to gobble the fish entrails tossed over the sides of the small fishing vessels docked near the pier in London.
    Dixce Bull had just passed his twentieth birthday and his fourth year of being apprenticed to the *Worshipful Company of Skinners* based out of London. The Worshipful Company was a livery company and the skinners traveled the world buying and trading for animal skins and furs, thus the name. It was a lucrative business and his older brother, Seth, was instrumental in getting him the apprenticeship.
    He spotted his mother, Anne and sister, Susan standing on the wharf. His mother looked concerned, as she wasn't thrilled with the idea of Dixce leaving home. But Susan cheerfully waved when she saw him looking their way. He heard his father's voice and turned to see him on board talking to the captain. Henry Bull was a wealthy man and he enjoyed being able to mingle with the captains in the *Worshipful* company. Dixce hoped to make his father proud with his new plans.

Dixce itched with excitement and couldn't stand still. He turned and watched the men loading the bulky boxes of supplies into the ship's hold. The hold would be bursting with supplies when they finished, enough to last the trip across the Atlantic Ocean to the New World. He waved when he spotted his friend John carrying a barrel of hard tack biscuits. John nodded and a huge grin spread over his face as he handed the barrel down to a man standing on a ladder below him. John moved out of the way as the man behind him leaned down to hand off a box. Supplies would continue to be passed down the line of men until the pile waiting on the dock was gone.

This would be Dixce's last trip aboard the huge galleon. When they finally arrived in Boston, Dixce would travel north to claim the parcel of land he'd been granted in York County in the new colony of Maine.

After saving all his wages for the last four years, Dixce planned to use the money to buy his own ship and sail the coasts of Maine buying furs. The Indians there were skilled fur trappers. The Maliseet, Micmac, Penobscot and Passamaquoddy Indians of Maine, known collectively as the Wabanaki or "People of the Dawnland", were friendly with traders. The northern furs were thick and plush, well sought after, especially beaver pelts. Dixce planned to start his own skinner business.

Seth came up and put his hand on his brother's shoulder. "This is a big day for ye," he said smiling. His dark beard was thicker than Dixce's and his hair almost black. He stood several inches taller and was three years older than Dixce.

Dixce turned and smiled. "Aye, and I have ye to thank for it. I kin hardly wait to get to Boston to look for me own ship."

"Best to hold that thought in check until this journey is over," warned Seth. "T'will take months to reach Boston."

Dixce nodded. "Thank ye for making it possible. With five more years left on me apprenticeship, without yer word I wouldn't be allowed to go out on me own."

Seth nodded. "Just remember to bring yer furs back to us for a good price."

Dixce nodded as the loud call of 'all hands on deck' floated through the air. The holds were closed and all the sailors lined up along the deck. He tugged his dark woolen jacket straight and stepped in line. The wool clothing he wore felt too warm under the sun, but out on the ocean it would barely feel thick enough.

Captain Solomon Willard appraised the men as he walked along the alert row. His blue uniform was neatly pressed and brand new. Dixce knew by the time Willard returned to England it would be worn and drab. But now the captain was an impressive sight with his neatly trimmed red beard and thick mustache. His blue eyes searched each of the crew for signs of illness or drunkenness. Such a man would become a burden on a long voyage.

Willard smiled and raised his hand in a salute. "Are ye ready to set sail, men?"

A chorus of "Ayes", "Yes, Sirs" yelled back at the captain.

"Then set the sails and off we'll be," said Captain Willard.

While the men climbed masts, raised the anchor and readied the vessel, Captain Willard climbed the steps to the forecastle, the elevated deck at the bow of the ship. He watched as the galleon slowly maneuvered its way through the few other vessels on this side of the port.

Willard was proud of this ship; it had made the trip to Boston numerous times with few problems. The *Golden Dove* was named for the rich golden color of the wood from which she was built. He hoped this trip would be as lucky. He knew of other vessels lost at sea in storms or raided by pirates. He'd faced storms before but so far never pirates.

As the vessel reached open waters, all four masts were raised and a strong wind carried them down river and away from the coast. The sailors' voices rose into a bawdy song as the vessel flew through the water. Captain Willard smiled as he hummed along with the off-key tune.

## Chapter 1
## Present Day Arkansas

James Ford stood in the doorway to the kitchen buttoning his pullover shirt. He smiled to himself as he observed his children sitting at the breakfast table. His daughter, eleven year-old Lily, was already a pretty little thing. Her curly chestnut hair reached her shoulders and she wore it pulled back with sparkly barrettes above her ears. She wore a pink t-shirt with a butterfly printed on the front and a pair of shorts. Right now she was gobbling blueberry pancakes, her favorite breakfast food, drinking gulps of milk between bites.

His stepson, Michel, was eighteen and graduating from high school in a few weeks. He was slim but with a toned body he kept in shape by running and cycling. He played on his high school basketball team and although not the star player, he scored points every game. He wore a red Razorback t-shirt and jeans. He wore his brown hair cut short to accommodate his bike helmet. Right now his dark brown eyes sparkled as he teased his little sister.

"You better slow down, Lily, or you're going to choke on those pancakes."

She frowned and her blue eyes flashed. "Will not," she said. But he noticed she did swallow slowly before taking another bite.

"Thanks, Mom. I need to get going if I'm to meet the guys before school," said Michel pushing out his chair. "Your pancakes are better than Denny's." That was high praise indeed as he loved Denny's breakfast menu.

Lacey turned away from the griddle where the next round of pancakes was sizzling. "Have a nice day," she said waving him over for the mandatory hug.

Michel was now five inches taller than his mother and he leaned down to give her a hug. "I'll be home after Tim and I study for the big Geometry test coming up on Monday. So don't wait dinner for me if I'm late," he said picking up his heavy blue denim backpack.

"I'll save you a plate," she said watching him leave before flipping over the pancakes.

James stepped back out of his way as Michel passed through the doorway.

"Bye, James," said Michel grinning. "Catch a crook today." Michel had stopped calling James 'Dad' when he turned seventeen. James figured it was his way of letting him know he wanted to be treated as a grownup. James didn't mind. Michel was a good kid, never caused his mother any trouble and kept his grades up all through school.

"See you later," said James. "Those pancakes smell good," he said to Lacey as he walked into the kitchen. The smell of pancakes and bacon hung heavy in the air.

Lacey turned off the griddle and piled the last round of pancakes on a serving plate. She wiped a bead of sweat off her brow. "I wasn't sure I'd made enough for us when Lily asked for thirds. But there's still plenty. Michel didn't eat his usual ten cakes this morning."

While she poured herself a glass of iced peppermint tea, James came up behind her. He brushed her wavy brown hair off the back of her neck and gave it a kiss.

She shivered. "That always gives me goose bumps," she said smiling. She handed him the plate of pancakes, picked up his glass of milk and followed him to the table.

James looked at Lily. "Honey, you have syrup on your chin."

Lily smiled. "I know. I'll wash it off in a minute." She turned to Lacey. "Can I have one more pancake, Mom?"

"I think you've had enough. Go brush your teeth and wash up before the school bus gets here," admonished Lacey.

Lily gave an exaggerated sigh. "OK. They were sure good." She hurried off and they watched her skip down the hall toward the bathroom.

"She's growing up too fast," complained James piling three pancakes on his plate. He reached for the bacon. "What am I going to do when she's a teenager? She's so pretty she'll attract boys like bees to pollen." He poured syrup on the pancake stack.

Lacey grinned. "You can invite her date inside and interview them while you clean your revolver." She reached for a pancake with her fork.

He nodded thoughtfully. "That's a great idea." He forked a big piece of pancake into his mouth and chewed, his grin widened as he imagined that future scenario and the frightened eyes of Lily's boyfriend.

Lily returned carrying her pink backpack. "Mom, did you remember to make my lunch today? I hate the stupid fish sticks they serve on Fridays."

"It's in the refrigerator," said Lacey.

Lily opened the door and pulled out her Wonder Woman lunch bag. "Thanks, Mom." She walked over and gave them each a hug. "See you later."

"Have a nice day," said Lacey.

Lily looked at her and grinned. "We get to watch a movie today."

James frowned. "How is that educational?"

Lily shrugged. "It is the end of the year, Dad. We always see movies. Bye."

They heard the front door slam as the bus horn honked out front.

"What grade is she in now?" asked James popping the last piece of bacon into his mouth.

"Sixth grade," laughed Lacey. "You never can remember. Seventh grade next year will be in the new Junior High they finished building this year."

He groaned. "It was never this hard raising Brad," he complained. "I didn't worry about him like I do Lily." His son Bradley was grown and married with his own son. He was the only child from James' first marriage.

After his wife died of cancer and James was shot while serving as a Bentonville Police Officer, he went through a period of depression while Bradley was a teenager. They leaned on each other to get through those years. James retired from the police force and became a private detective before he met Lacey. In fact they met when her mother hired James to find her. Lacey had run away after accidentally shooting her sister-in-law, fearful she would go to prison. James rescued her from a serial rapist.

Now they'd been married over twelve years, but to him sometimes it seemed like only twelve months. Time went by so fast.

Lacey looked at her husband while she cleared the table and he read the newspaper on his iPad. More gray was appearing around the temples in his short brown hair and it made him look distinguished. As she watched, he raised his head a little to read the small print through his bi-focals. He was still slim, with broad shoulders even though he was turning fifty-two in another week, he didn't look it. She tried not to think about it. That meant she was going to be forty-two on her birthday. Definitely middle aged. She'd pulled out a gray hair last week and she hoped she wouldn't find any more for a while.

"You can enlarge the print size on that thing, you know," she teased.

He blinked his brown eyes and ignored her remark.

"What are you working on today?"

"I'm finishing up the paperwork for Mrs. Warren," he said. "We should get paid by the end of the week."

"This is the end of the week," she said smiling. "Today is Friday, remember?"

"Oh." He looked perplexed. "That's right. The weeks go by so fast."

"School will be out in two weeks. Have you decided where we should go for a family vacation?"

"Not really. I know the kids want some place with a beach. And you like shopping. That doesn't really narrow it down very much," he complained.

"I got a letter from my cousin, Annette Prescott. She wants us to come to visit in Maine. She lives in Thomaston, right on the coast."

His eyes widened. "That's a long drive."

"I know. It's about four days drive from here. But we could fly." She sat back down at the table. "I checked our frequent flyer miles and we have enough for three round trip adult tickets. We'd just have to pay for Lily," she explained. "We've earned a lot of miles flying to Germany and all around for your work over the last few years. They'll expire if we don't use them soon."

"We'd have to rent a car besides a place to stay," he murmured thoughtfully. "But we could do it, if you think the kids would like it there."

"Annette says she has a car we could borrow for day trips. And the kids would love it," she said. "I haven't been there since I was a teenager, but there are a lot of great things to do. There's whale watching and the beach, of course. And Old Orchard Beach with the carnival and pier are only an hour away. Plus there are lots of great seafood places to eat."

He smiled. "Sounds like you have it all planned out."

"Only if you want to go."

"I've never been that far northeast. It sounds fun."

"Great, I'll call Annette and tell her to expect us. She has a friend who rents cabins in Rockland, she said she could reserve one for us."

He nodded and went back to reading. When she wasn't looking he enlarged the print on his iPad.

Chapter 2
Maine Coast 1632

Dixce stared with pride at the shallop. New paint spelled out her name in white letters on the side of the small sailing vessel; *Merry Wanderer*. It wasn't a fancy ship but with his crew of ten sailors it was a promising start to what he hoped would become a thriving skinner business in this new land. His land grant in York County, Maine made him a landholder and there weren't many men who could claim that at the young age of twenty-one years.

He boarded his vessel and ordered the men to prepare to leave the dock. This trip had been successful and the hold was stuffed with furs, mostly beaver pelts that would bring a good price in Boston. His last cargo had brought him even more than expected. And these pelts were full and thick winter pelts from Canadian beavers.

Dixce wasn't surprised when he'd been able to talk his friend John Henley into joining him as First Mate on the *Merry Wanderer*. He'd known John for five years and knew him to be an honest and loyal friend. Dixce was willing to share his hoped for wealth with his hard working friend.

John nodded his approval at the crew as they finished storing the food supplies below deck. He stood with his hands on his hips and surveyed the sky. The weather looked promising for this trip. He held up one stout finger and felt the steady breeze. Good sailing weather to be sure.

"Ready to set sail, Captain," he called loudly to Dixce.
"Give the order then," answered Dixce.

John smiled and began calling out orders to weigh anchor and set a sail to get them out of the harbor. John shaded his eyes against the sunrise glare as he watched the men. John was shorter but more muscular than most of the men. They knew not to give him any guff. He looked like an ancient Viking with the sun shining off his almost white, blond hair and beard. He was a hard taskmaster but always fair and the men knew it.

They set sail as the sun was rising in the east. Most of his crew was older than Dixce. He had problems with that at first when he tried to hire sailors. But the sight of cash money had changed a few minds and he was happy with the men who worked for him.

"Captain, the wind's fair, we should make Boston in three days," said John.

"I believe yer right." Dixce watched the coastline as they passed through Penobscot Bay. "Looks to be a right clear day." Only a few white clouds scuttled through the blue sky. Dixce silently laughed to himself at being called 'Captain' by his best friend. But John insisted they be formal in front of the crew.

"Off the port bow!" called a sailor from his perch high on the main mast. "Must be ten of 'em! What a sight!"

Dixce shielded his eyes from the sun and spotted the pod of humpback whales in the distance. A waterspout shot high into the air as one of the bigger whales blew. The entire crew was so engrossed in watching the whales no one noticed the small pinnace rowing up from behind until it was too late.

Dixce was taken completely by surprise when a loud thump echoed through the air as the smaller vessel bumped into the side of his ship.

Suddenly there were French men climbing over the side, guns leveled at the crew.

"Atendez!" shouted a tall burly man with a loaded flintlock pistol pointed directly at Dixce. Six other men stood behind their leader. They were all dark-skinned from years in the sun with dirty bandanas wrapped around their heads, bare chests and short torn-off breeches. One man had a white scar running down his leathery cheek. Another was missing two fingers on his left hand. The leader's gold tooth glimmered in the sun as he sneered at Dixce. They all looked dangerous.

Stepping closer and pointing his pistol at Dixce's face, the leader indicted for the men to raise their hands. "Give furs and food," he said in broken English. His wicked smile showed several missing teeth and his eyes glittered menacingly. Shaggy black hair hung down to his shoulders and he wore a silver chain and cross around his neck.

When the sailors were slow to raise their hands in the air, the pirate stepped closer to Dixce and put the pistol barrel against his temple.

"Do what he says," shouted John. What else could they do? They were taken completely by surprise. The sailors raised their hands and the pirates collected pistols and knives from them.

The pirates tied Dixce and John to a mast and ordered the rest of the crew to sit down against the bulkhead walls. After opening the hatch to the hold, three pirates began throwing up bundles and boxes to the two men waiting on deck. It took them barely twenty minutes to unload the *Merry Wanderer* with all that their small wooden pinnace could hold.

The robbers laughed and gave a jaunty salute as they jumped over the ship's side onto the pinnace. The pirate leader waved as the men rowed away and he called out loudly, "Merci!"

Dixce felt like screaming or crying, but as the captain he would do neither. One of his men hurriedly untied him and John.

"Sorry, Capt'n," he apologized. "Didn't seem as we had much choice."

"No, reckon not," mumbled Dixce. He looked down into the bowels of the ship at the almost empty hold. "Let's see if we can find the slimy buggers. Turn this ship around!"

By the time the ship was turned, the pinnace was nowhere on the horizon. The pirates had slipped into one of the many small coves that dotted the Maine coastline. Most likely they'd rowed up stream on a river to a secret hideout.

Dixce's anger and temper grew with every mile they sailed. He'd counted on the money from those furs to trade for his next load of goods. Now he barely had enough to pay the men their meager wages for three days work.

"What de ya think you'll do now, Captain?" asked John, shaking his head sadly. "They took most of our food, too. Don't know that we have enough to feed the men before we can reach Boston."

"Don't rightly know yet," answered Dixce. "I need to ponder on it."

After several hours with no luck at finding the thieves, Dixce did his first dishonest thing. He plundered two small trading vessels to restock his food supplies and headed to Boston.

###

Over the next few months Dixce tried to gain recourse though the Boston courts, but the French refused to acknowledge guilt when they claimed to have no affiliation with the pirates. His anger made him bold and he assembled a crew of fifteen men and decided if he couldn't beat them, he would join them.

At first Dixce tried raiding French sailing vessels, but they offered little to steal. Instead he began robbing the richer English vessels. This was much more satisfactory and profitable. Dixce and his men spent the next few months robbing ships and raiding coastal villages, earning him the title of the "Dread Pirate". Not only was he gathering goods, but gold bullion and anything else of value he fancied.

Dixce Bull's most daring raid happened in late 1632 when he attacked the trading station built at the mouth of the Damariscotta River at Pemaquid, Maine. The trading station was a center for fish processing and consisted of about eighty-five families and a trading post. No other thieves had dared to raid the prosperous, well-defended town.

"Are ye ready?" hollered Dixce to his men as they approached the harbor.

Grinning from ear to ear, the men answered back, "Aye, Capt'n".

Sailing into the harbor at dawn, Dixce's ship opened fire and came in with guns blazing. The loud booms and crashes, the smoke and flames woke the sleeping town. His men stormed ashore and took the post with virtually no resistance. Screams echoed through the morning air as Dixce's crew broke into homes and looted any thing of value. The frightened citizens cowered in their nightclothes and prayed to be left alive. The whispers of the "Dread Pirate Dixce" swept through the town as people ran for safety.

Dixce's men looted the place of five hundred pounds of goods and sacked the town, torching buildings on their way out. Booty seized that day amounted to thousands of dollars, a veritable fortune in 1632.

The only resistance came as they were sailing away. Shots came at them from on shore and although only a few bullets made it as far as the ship, one of them struck John. Red blood blossomed on the front of his shirt as he fell to the deck.

John looked up, fear darkening his hazel eyes. "Looks like I'm done for," he mumbled.

Dixce rushed to his side, but the wound was horrific. There was no way to save his friend and John died in Dixce's arms. John's death took all the joy out of their raid as the men stood around Dixce in silence.

They sailed away from Pemaquid with heavy hearts. Pirating didn't seem exciting to any of them any more.

When Dixce's men next raided a ship from Salem, Massachusetts, the captain later reported to authorities that the pirates were still unnerved by the death of their mate.

Governor Winthrop dispatched a small squadron of ships to hunt down Dixce and the pirates, but they were never found. Unbeknownst to the New World, Dixce gave up pirating and returned to England where he finished out his apprenticeship as a skinner.

******

HISTORICAL NOTE:

Dixce Bull was the first recorded pirate to haunt the shores of Maine for approximately two years before he disappeared. Some Maine legends say he was killed, but proof exists that he returned to England and finished out his apprenticeship with the skinner company. Genealogy records his parents as Henry Bull and Anne. Only two siblings are known, Seth and Susan. I have used fanciful fiction to tell his story but it is based on recorded facts.

Pirate legend says Dixce buried some of his ill-gotten treasure. Folks in Maine still believe the Dread Pirate Dixce Bull left behind booty on Damariscove Island and Cushings Island. But it seems that so far no one has ever found any.

## Chapter 3
## Present Day

Lily watched wide-eyed as a plane landed on the runway. She was so excited to go on her first airplane flight she'd hardly slept the night before. She adjusted the strap of her pink backpack on her shoulder.

"When is it our turn, Mom?" she asked Lacey coming up to the seats where her family waited for their flight to be called.

The Northwest Arkansas Regional Airport was small compared to most, but it was thrilling enough for Lily. She'd been solemn as they went through the airport security process of checking their luggage and being x-rayed. Now she practically wiggled with excitement at the thoughts of flying. "Is it much longer?" she asked.

"According to the information board we have fifteen more minutes before they start boarding the plane," answered Lacey. She smiled at Lily hoping this vacation would meet all her expectations.

Lily sighed and sat down next to her mother. She smoothed her hands down her new blue Capri pants and straightened the front of her favorite yellow t-shirt. She looked at her brother and wondered how he could calmly play a game on his iPhone. While she fidgeted with her purse, she people-watched. There were men in business suits and others in gaudy colored Hawaiian print shirts sitting next to women in dresses and others in shorts so short her mother wouldn't even let her wear them. She wondered where they were all going.

She figured not all of them were flying to Maine as everyone at this gate had to change planes in Atlanta, Georgia. Only some would be heading to Portland, Maine. It all seemed amazing to her. She fiddled with the zipper on her purse and watched as a plane took off. How did something so huge manage to stay in the air? she wondered.

Finally the call came to start boarding their flight. They had to wait as the first class passengers and those who needed help boarded. Lily watched a woman with two little children being helped by a man in a blue uniform. He pushed a stroller while she carried a baby and her carry-on bag.

When it was their turn to board she stayed right beside her mother as they walked down a long hallway and stepped onto the plane. The stewardess smiled and welcomed them and asked if they knew how to find their seats.

Lacey nodded, before carrying her small carry-on suitcase and purse down the narrow aisle to their seats. "This is it," she told Lily. "You take the seat by the window while I put this bag in the overhead compartment."

Lily gladly took the window seat. She wanted to see how high they flew and quickly began peering out the little round window. Men were loading luggage into the plane. Some of them tossed the bags onto a conveyor belt. Lily winced. She hoped no one had packed anything breakable in those suitcases. She spotted her purple bag as it landed on the conveyor belt then disappeared inside the open hatch.

James and Michel each stowed their carry-on and took seats across the aisle. Michel took the window seat and shoved his phone in his pocket. He hadn't wanted to admit it, but even he was excited to go on his first airplane flight. He settled himself into the seat and pulled at the neck of his red Arkansas Razorback t-shirt. He was outgrowing this one, but it was his favorite.

"Please fasten your seatbelts," said the pretty stewardess. "You may refer to the booklet in the pocket in front of you to follow along with safety instructions." She proceeded to explain about seatbelts, how the chair cushions were floatable in the event of a crash over water, and how the oxygen masks would drop down in an emergency. "Smoking is not allowed on any flight," she said sternly.

Lily's eyes widened when she heard that adults were to put on their own oxygen masks before helping others.

Lacey looked at her and smiled. "Don't worry, I wouldn't forget to help you with your mask," she whispered. "Nothing bad is going to happen."

When the stewardess finished talking she sat down and the captain spoke over the loudspeaker telling them how long the flight would take and at what altitude they would be flying. Then the plane began to move. Lily watched as they drove to the runway and took their place in line to take off. There was only one plane in front of them. All of a sudden the plane sped up and she felt herself being pushed back into her seat.

Lacey put her hand over Lily's on the armrest. Lily was gripping so tightly her knuckles were white. She looked at her mother and smiled as the plane left the ground.

Lily watched out the window as the ground receded and everything below them got smaller, and smaller. Soon the cars on the highway looked like toys. They flew over farms with tiny black and brown cows; long chicken houses and buildings that began to look smaller than the houses in her Monopoly game.

Suddenly they broke through thick white clouds. The sun shone in her face through the window and she sat back in her seat. Now all she could see were white fluffy clouds below them. "Darn it, I can't see anything down there now," she complained to Lacey.

"Probably not until we get ready to land," said her mother.

Lily folded her arms across her chest and pouted.

"Here, you can use my phone to play a game." Lacey handed her an iPhone. "Just don't try to make a phone call. I know you'll be tempted to call Cindy."

Lily nodded, although she would have liked to call her best friend to brag a little. She touched icons on the small screen and pulled up one of the games her mother installed on her phone for Lily to use. Before she started her game she looked across the aisle at Michel. He was already engrossed in a game on his phone.

While Lily played, Lacey pulled the in-flight magazine from the pocket in front of her seat. It described all kinds of amazing and ridiculous things you could buy and she liked to see what was offered, not that she would spend that kind of money on something so frivolous.

The flight took over two hours and by the second one, Lily had gotten bored and dozed off in her seat. The stewardess handed out only drinks and cookies, and Lacey didn't wake Lily to eat hers.

Their layover at the Atlanta airport lasted ninety minutes giving them time to buy lunch and find their next gate. The second flight was longer and Lily slept through most of it once the plane flew above the clouds. When they descended to land in Portland, Lacey woke her to see the ocean. Dark blue water with tiny boats passed below the plane.

"Wow, Mom, the runway is right next to the water," exclaimed Lily, her eyes wide. "Do you think any planes have ever landed in the ocean?"

Lacey laughed. "I don't think so."

The plane bumped as it hit the runway and began slowing down. Lily giggled and looked out the window at the other planes. "Yea," she whispered to herself. "We're finally here."

The stewardess warned everyone to remain seated with seatbelts fastened until the plane stopped at their gate.

"We'll let most everyone off first," said James from across the aisle. "No sense standing in line for fifteen minutes until they open the door."

As soon as the plane stopped, people jumped up and began dragging their carry-on out of the overhead bins, then rushed to get in the aisle. They stood there for over ten minutes before the door opened on the side of the plane and they began to disembark.

"Daddy was right," said Lily looking up at her mother. "Why was everyone in such a hurry to just stand in the line?"

"I don't know, but it's always like that. Maybe some are afraid they'll miss a connecting flight or something. Your Dad and I wait until the line thins out before we get up."

When there were only a few other passengers left, the Fords stood up to leave.

The stewardess and copilot thanked them for choosing to fly Delta as they exited.

When they reached the baggage claim area in the Portland airport they waited twenty minutes before their luggage finally rode by on the metal carousel. Michel was quick to find each one and he managed to grab them on the first pass despite the crowd.

Lacey's cousin, Annette greeted them as they turned to leave the area.

"Sorry I'm so late," she said breathlessly rushing to hug Lacey. "There was a lot of traffic this evening."

Lacey hugged her back. "You're not late, we just now got our suitcases."

Annette looked at the others. "Hi, nice to finally meet everyone. Lacey keeps me updated with Christmas cards and photos. I would have recognized all of you." She looked at Lily. "Except maybe you. You've grown so much!"

Lily smiled and held out her hand. "Nice to meet you…" she looked at her mother. "What shall I call her? She's not my cousin, is she?"

"I'm your second cousin," said Annette.

Lily looked confused.

"Never mind. Just call me Annette."

Lily smiled. "OK, Miss Annette."

Annette looked questioningly at Lacey.

"It's a Southern thing," laughed Lacey.

"I'm parked out front in the loading area so we better get moving before the car gets towed," said Annette smiling.

They hurried out of the building and loaded the luggage in the back of a big white SUV. "This is the car I drive in the winter because of all the snow," said Annette. "It has four-wheel drive. But I have a Camry you can use for traveling around. I brought this one because I didn't think the Camry would hold all your luggage."

"That's nice of you to loan us a car," said James climbing in the back seat with Lily after loading the luggage in the car.

"Well, the Camry's old, but it runs good. And it uses less gas than this big thing," said Annette pulling out into the traffic lane. "It'll take about an hour and a half to get to Thomaston. But I'll leave the highway for a while so you can view the scenic route by the ocean."

"That will be nice," said Lacey settling in the front passenger seat.

"I figured since you hadn't eaten dinner," said Annette. "We could stop in Freeport where there's a wicked good seafood restaurant. You can get a two lobster dinner for under twenty dollars."

"That sounds like my kind of place," said Michel excitedly from the back third row seat. "I've been waiting to taste lobster."

"You've never eaten lobster?" asked Annette surprised.

"Nope. It's too expensive back home."

"Oh. It's just so common up here," said Annette. "Years ago the inmates in the Thomaston prison ate lobster three times a week because it was plentiful and cheap. They started complaining about it. Personally, I think it's wicked good and would love to eat some every week. But the prices have gone up even here."

Lily looked at her father. "What's wicked good mean?" she whispered.

"That's how people in Maine say something is really good."

"Oh."

"You'll hear the word 'wicked' a lot," said James smiling.

Lily turned away and pressed her face against the car window as she gazed at the ocean, the beach and all the lobster boats. "Wow, this is going to be a great vacation."

## Chapter 4
## Present day Maine

The first two days of vacation went by quickly. Lacey loved the little rental cabin. It only had two small bedrooms, but there was a loft over the living room. Michel claimed it for himself rather than bunk in with Lily. The owners supplied them with a blow-up mattress and he loved it. There was a small kitchen with all the appliances, a breakfast nook and a living room furnished with three chairs, a sofa that could be opened to a bed and a coffee table. Colorful rag rugs covered parts of the wooden floor. A small porch had two Adirondack chairs facing the ocean.

They'd already established a bit of a routine. Lacey stocked the kitchen with cereals and granola bars, fresh fruit, milk and juice for breakfast. They ate lunch while they were out sight seeing and Annette insisted on making dinner each night. She said she loved having visitors.

After they ate breakfast, Lacey took Lily down to the beach. When the tide was high the cabin sat less than fifty feet from the small rocky beach area. They were on a hill and ten steps led down to the shore. Right at the edge of the water there was a little yellow sand and lots of tide pools.

Even in the summer on hot days, the ocean water was a chilly, between fifty and sixty degrees Fahrenheit. Lily didn't seem to mind the cold water but Lacey only got her feet wet. They spent the morning searching for hermit crabs in the tide pools or hunting for sea glass at the edge of the tide. Mostly they found the common white or brown sand-etched glass, but once Lily found a rare piece of dark red glass. Exploring the tide pools kept her busy until the others were ready to go sightseeing.

By the time they came back inside to change, James and Michel were awake and eating breakfast around ten o'clock.

"Hi, Daddy," called Lily running up to the small breakfast table. "Look what I found today." She held out her hand to show him the tiny white sand dollar resting on her palm.

"Wow, that's really nice."

"I'm going to put it with the other shells I'm saving to take home." She already had a small box half full of spiral cast-off snail shells, clamshells and sea glass.

"When it's time to go home you'll have to pick out your favorites," he warned. "You can only take home one small box of shells."

She grimaced. "I know. And no live hermit crabs."

"Definitely not," he said before finishing his orange juice. He looked over at Lacey, smiled and winked.

Lacey patted Lily's shoulder. "Go rinse off the salt water in the shower and get dressed. Annette is taking us to Boothbay Harbor today."

"I'll hurry, that sounds fun."

"So what's special about Boothbay?" asked Michel, finishing his third bowl of cereal.

"I love going there. They have this really great store with all kinds of unusual things for sale. Like fairies, mermaids, chimes, swords, magical stuff and clothing like you would wear to a medieval festival. There is always some soft 'new age' music playing and they sell CD's and posters and jewelry and just wicked neat stuff," she said laughing. "I loved going there when I visited Maine as a teenager. The floor is covered in glitter and I don't know, it's just great."

"Wow," laughed Michel. "I don't think I've ever seen you this excited about shopping."

Lily was dressed when Annette arrived. She brought the SUV to make sure they had room for everyone. It was her day off at the hospital where she worked as a nurse, and she wanted to enjoy the day as a tourist with them. Even her son, Winston, was coming with them.

The boys quickly grabbed the backseat and began talking. Winston was a twenty-three year old with long red hair he wore in a ponytail and bright green eyes. He was taller than Michel, with broad shoulders and muscular arms. He owned a small boat and worked pulling his own lobster traps. They two young men hit it off right away and Michel thought Winston was the coolest guy he'd ever met.

"So where do you want to go first?" asked Annette as she drove down Route 1.

"To *Enchantments*," said Lacey grinning.

Annette laughed. "I might have known. That was our favorite place in Boothbay."

"We spent hours looking at everything," agreed Lacey. "Stuff is so jammed together a person could spend days in there and not see everything."

It took forty-five minutes to reach the end of the peninsula. Lily's eyes scanned all the wonderful sights as they drove into town. "Mom, I saw a sign for the Maine State Aquarium. Can we go there?"

"If you want to. It's a fun place, too."

"Hey, Mom," called Michel from the back seat. "Winston said there are boats in the harbor to take tourists out whale watching. Could we go on one?"

Lacey frowned. "It takes about four hours to go out and back, I don't know."

"I've an idea," said James. "Why don't you girls go shopping, to the aquarium and have lunch while we go whale watching?"

Lacey smiled. "That's a great idea. You could call me when the boat returns to the dock."

"Thanks, James," said Michel, giving him a fist bump.

"I don't mind going out with you two. It's better than following your Mom around carrying her packages," whispered James.

Annette dropped the men off at the harbor entrance to the boats and drove up a steep hill to park by *Enchantments*.

Lily's eyes popped in wonder as she gazed in amazement at the front of the store. *Enchantments* was a long building painted bright pink with multicolored flags hanging across the front. The grassy yard out front held all types of garden decorations; cars and tractors with spinning wheels, birds, windmills and brightly colored bugs with flapping cloth wings.

They quickly crossed the street and went inside past big glass globes and wind chimes tinkling in the breeze. There was a thick layer of shiny glittery bits all over the floor. Glass cases held crystals, figurines of mythical creatures and lots of jewelry. The back of the store held shelves of books, some about how to tell fortunes or read tarot cards. They walked down aisle after aisle of amazing things, then went upstairs to see clothing and more items.

James phoned to let them know they'd left the dock and were on "Cap'n Fish's Cruise" and they would be back around two o'clock.

It was close to noon by the time Lily made up her mind which small fairy doll she wanted to buy and Lacey picked out a necklace with a piece of dark blue sea glass. They left the store and headed down the street to a small café for lunch.

After they were seated at a table with a checked red and white oilcloth tablecloth, Lily looked at her mother. "You were right, Mom. That store was the best ever! I wish we had one like that in Bentonville."

The women ordered seafood salads and Lily had a hamburger. After lunch they returned to the car and headed toward the other side of the town to West Boothbay Harbor and the Maine State Aquarium.

Lily stared in fascination at all the fish, starfish, sea cucumbers and lobsters in the aquarium tanks. They all walked the halls and stared into the tanks, reading the signs telling about the creatures inside. They were standing around the touch tank when Lacey's phone rang.

"Hey, Lace, we should be docking at the harbor in twenty minutes. We had a great time. The boys are still talking about the small pod of humpback whales we spotted," said James.

"OK, we'll meet you in the parking lot."

"Lily you only have a few more minutes here. If you want to touch something in the tank, you have to be brave now," Lacey informed her.

Lily took a deep breath and slowly put her hand into the cool water of the tank. She ran her fingers carefully over the edge of a sea urchin.

"It feels funny," she giggled. She was about to touch the sea cucumber when it squirted water at her. A tiny stream shot out of the water and splashed the front of her shirt. She jumped back and started laughing. "I peed on me!"

The employee guarding the tank and educating the patrons grinned at Lily. "It's not pee. They do that all the time. It scares off predators and helps them move away."

Lily was still laughing while her mother wiped at her shirt with a tissue. "Daddy will think this is funny," she quipped.

"I'm sure he will," agreed Lacey. "It's time to go." She turned to the employee. "I bet this is a fun place to work."

He grinned. "It is. Have a great day and come back any time."

They arrived at the parking lot by the dock as James and the boys stepped off the boat. Michel spotted them and waved excitedly, hurrying across the parking lot as the other men followed him.

"Mom, that was amazing! We saw six humpback whales and one was a baby," he said. "And a seal followed beside the boat in the water for a while. And the sea gulls were fun to watch. It was great. I really like being out on the water."

Lacey smiled. "I'm glad you had a good time."

Lily held up her fairy doll. "Look what I got." The little blond haired fairy wore a pink skirt and had lavender gauze wings.

"That's nice," said Michel leaning down to look at the toy. "Did you spill something on your shirt?" he teased.

She laughed. "No, a sea cucumber spit at me!"

"We went to the aquarium after lunch," explained Lacey.

"And we saw a blue lobster!" said Lily. "Dark blue all over. Can you believe it?"

"When I was working on my boat I caught one in a lobster trap one time," said Winston in his deep voice. "They look pretty wicked. I let it go after taking a picture. I didn't want anyone to eat it."

Lily stared at him in awe. "Wow! You have your own boat?"

"He does," interrupted Michel turning to his mother. "Winston said I could go out with him tomorrow to check his traps. Can I go?"

Lacey frowned and looked at James.

"Michel's a good swimmer and he'll wear a life jacket," said James. "They already talked about it on the cruise. I think it would be all right."

"Mrs. Ford, I'll take good care of him. I started lobstering with my dad when I was twelve; I have lots of experience. And I don't go too far from shore," said Winston.

Lacey nodded. "I guess it would be all right. He can see how hard the work is to catch lobsters. He certainly likes to eat them."

Michel grabbed his mother and lifted her off the ground in a hug. "Thanks, Mom!"

"I'll save some of my catch for all of us to have for dinner tomorrow," promised Winston. "I go out pretty early so we'll have to leave before six o'clock."

After piling into the car they pulled out of the parking lot. They stopped for some sandwiches at a little food stand, as the men hadn't eaten lunch. It was a quiet ride back to Rockland. Everyone was tired but happy.

## Chapter 5

Michel was so excited about going out with Winston on the boat that he was awake by five o'clock without an alarm. Lacey found him in the kitchen dressed and eating cereal.

"Do you need me to pack a lunch?" she asked, rubbing the sleep from her eyes.

"Nah, Winston said he would pick up some sandwiches at the store where he buys his bait for the traps. He'll probably get water and soda, too," said Michel between bites. "But could I take a couple of bottles of juice?"

"Sure, that's OK. I have to go to the grocery store to restock today anyway. You can take the last few bottles except one orange juice for James' breakfast."

Michel poured himself another half bowl of frosted shredded wheat and added milk.

"You'll be extra careful out there today, won't you?"

Michel looked at his mother and nodded. "I know you worry, but I'll wear a life vest and be extra careful. Winston already told me about some of the accidents other fishermen have had. I won't do anything stupid."

"I know. I'm a mom after all, I just worry."

There was a soft knock on the door and she went to answer it.

"Good morning, Mrs. Ford," said Winston. He knew what she was thinking. "I promise to watch out for him and bring him back in one piece."

She smiled. "Thanks."

Michel came up behind her and gave her a hug. "See you later, Mom."

She watched from the front porch as the two of them climbed into Winston's old gray pickup truck and drove away.

"Your mom seems like a worrier," said Winston glancing at Lacey in the window.

"Well, yeah she is. But we've had some pretty weird things happen before, so I guess she has good reason to be a worrier," admitted Michel.

"Yeah, like what?"

"Well, my sister was kidnapped once, and James has been shot twice," said Michel.

Winston glanced at him. "Holy smokes, I guess that would make her nervous."

"I can't believe the sun's so far up already," said Michel looking at the sky.

"We're so far north the sun rises around four-thirty this time of year."

Winston slowed the truck and turned down a steep hill to reach the little Rockport Harbor and dock. After he parked he pulled a cooler out from behind the front seat. "I got plenty of sandwiches and bottles of water," he said putting the cooler down on the sidewalk next to the truck. "I have to get the bait bucket out of the back."

"I brought some juice, just in case we get really thirsty," said Michel, holding up a plastic grocery bag. "Thanks for taking me out. I'll try not to get in your way."

"No problem," said Winston, hefting a metal pail over the tailgate and setting it on the ground. "I get lonely out here by myself sometime. Dad and I used to lobster together."

Michel picked up the cooler and Winston carried the pail leading the way down to the dock where four boats floated tied off the dock. Michel pointed to a sailboat at the end of the pier. "That's a nice boat."

Winston grinned. "That's a windjammer. It's the schooner *Heron* owned by Capt. Twig. He takes tourists out for day cruises along the Maine coast to see lighthouses and puffins."

"What's a puffin?"

"It's a funny looking fat black bird with a white stomach and wedge shaped orange beak and orange feet. They nest on some of the small islands on the coast," explained Winston. He stopped in front of a lobster boat. "Here's my boat."

Winston's boat was painted white and thirty feet long. It had what looked like a cabin toward the bow and the sides were taller at the front than the back. Winston took the cooler from Michel while he climbed onto the boat, then handed it and the bait bucket to him before untying the ropes attached to the dock. He jumped aboard and landed with a thump.

"I named my boat *Chelsea Two*. My dad had *Chelsea One*. I'll start the engine and you can look around," said Winston moving inside the cabin to the steering wheel.

Michel noticed a long pole with a hook on the end lying on the deck. There was a built-in storage area at the back of the boat. He lifted the lid and saw weird looking clothing inside. He put the lid back down and sat on top as the boat began to move.

It took about twenty minutes to get to the area where Winston's small buoys floated on top of the water. There were dozens of different colored buoys in this area. Winston stopped the boat, dropped the anchor and walked back to Michel.

"Now comes the working part," he said smiling. He opened the back storage bin and pulled out two pairs of what looked like thick overalls. They were waterproof and had a bulky front and back below the straps. "We're going to put these on over our clothes." He handed one to Michel.

"I wondered why you only wore shorts," said Michel. "It's already chilly out here on the water." He sat down on the bin and pushed his feet into the legs of the overalls. "Do we wear a life jacket over this?"

Winston grinned. "Used to have to. But these were invented in 2019. They have float material inside the bib and back. Most fishermen refused to wear lifejackets because they're bulky and get in the way when you work. So some of them drown each year. These suits replace the life jacket and are not too bulky. Don't know why someone didn't think of this years ago." He handed Michel a pair of thick rubber boots. "Put these on instead of your shoes to keep your feet dry."

After they were suited up, he said, "We'll pull up my traps now and see if we caught any bugs." He smiled. "That's what Mainers call lobsters." Winston picked up the hooked pole and used it to retrieve one of the floating buoys. "This is called a gaff," he said as he pulled the float toward the side of the boat.

"Are all of those floating things yours?" asked Michel.

"Nah, mine are the ones with a white top, blue bottom and yellow stripe around the middle. Each lobsterman has their own color-coded buoys with a registration number on them," Winston grunted as he pulled the lobster trap from the water. The metal trap dripped water into the boat as he set it on the deck. He laughed. "This is why you need rubber boots."

Michel walked closer and looked at the trap. It was made of green plastic-coated metal wire with funny funnel-shaped webbing inside. There was one lobster inside and two small fish flopping in the bottom.

Winston pointed to the trap. "This part is called the kitchen where I put the bait. The lobsters crawl through that funnel shaped mesh thing and can't get back out. That's called the parlour. Looks like we've only got one bug this time." He reached inside and picked up the lobster. "You have to grab them like this behind their head on top of their body so they can't pinch you with their claws." He proceeded to measure the lobster. "To keep a lobster the body has to be at least three and a fourth inches on the dorsal part not including the head, but less than five inches."

"How come you can't keep the big ones over five inches?"

"Because they're breeders. If we harvested the big ones, there wouldn't be any babies next year. You also can't keep females carrying eggs or ones with a notched tail showing they've been caught before carrying eggs."

"Wow, lobstering is a lot more complicated than I thought. So we can keep this one?"

Winston nodded and showed him how to tell this was a male and that it was four inches. He then popped elastic bands on the lobster's claws to keep him from pinching. "Now he goes in this container that has cold sea water in it so he doesn't die before we can get him back to shore." He removed the lid on a big blue plastic bin and dropped the lobster inside.

"What do you do with the fish that got caught in the trap?" asked Michel.

"Usually toss it back unless I can use it for bait. If it's a small mackerel, I'll keep it. The next step is to check the bait bag." He picked up the live fish and tossed them back in the water.

Winston pulled a little mesh bag out of the trap and looked at it. "Needs to be refilled with chum." He took two pieces of cut up fish and guts out of the bait bucket and wrapped it in the mesh bag then hung it back inside the trap and threw the trap back into the water. "Now we'll go to the next trap. I don't usually drop the anchor each time I grab a trap but I figured I'd take my time and show you everything I do."

For the rest of the morning Winston drove the boat from one floating buoy to another. While the boat floated on the water he swiftly yanked a buoy, pulled out and measured any lobsters in the trap and refilled bait as needed. Michel was amazed at how efficiently Winston worked.

"Do you want to try one?" asked Winston. "We'll stop here so you can pull these two traps, then we'll eat lunch."

Michel was a little clumsy with the gaff at first but he managed to pull in both floating buoys without falling overboard. The watery traps were heavier than he thought because Winston made it look easy. Michel gingerly picked up the lobsters and Winston helped him measure them and put on the rubber bands. They had to throw one lobster back that was too small and one female with a notched tail. But that still left three lobsters to keep.

"Hey man, you did good," complimented Winston. "You'll make a good lobsterman yet! You can pull more traps after lunch."

They washed their hands off in the ocean and sat down to eat lunch. Michel was starving by now and realized his shoulders would be sore by the time they finished the day.

"So," said Winston thoughtfully. "Does your dad mind if you call him James?"

Michel swallowed a big bite of ham sandwich and grinned. "Nah, he's my step-dad. I called him dad when I was younger."

"Do you ever get to see your real dad?"

Michel shook his head. "After my folks got divorced he moved away. I haven't heard from him in fifteen years. I don't even know where he is." He shrugged. "He wasn't a very nice man. I think my mom was relieved when he moved away."

"So James married your mom and they had Lily?"

"Yeah. She's pretty cute most of the time. James used to be a cop and was married before. His son, Brad, is about your age. He's married and has a kid. Mom told me James' first wife died of cancer. The next year James got shot and almost died. He never went back to being a cop, but now he's a private detective. He got shot doing that once, too."

"Sounds like he still lives dangerously." Winston started on his second sandwich.

"Mom said your dad died. What happened?"

Winston frowned.

"You don't have to tell me if you don't want to," said Michel.

"No. It's just that he turned up missing one day out checking his traps. The coast guard hunted for days, but all they found was some of his gear from the boat floating in the water. They said he drowned, but they never found his body," said Winston. "That was two years ago."

"Wow, I'm sorry."

Winston shrugged. "At first mom was against me buying this boat and taking over some of dad's traps. But she finally gave in. I do pretty well most years. But I'm taking a few college courses to get a degree in business management. I figured if something happened and I couldn't do this anymore, I'd have something to fall back on."

"That's a smart idea. I'm heading to college this fall at the University of Arkansas. I'm not sure what to major in yet," said Michel. "Guess I'll eventually decide."

"You know, there was one strange thing about my dad going missing. The floating debris from his boat was near Damariscove Island and he didn't have any lobster traps out there."

"Huh, that is weird. Why do you think he would have been out there?"

Winston sighed. "He'd gotten this idea there was pirate treasure on that island. Maybe he went to look for it. I wasn't feeling good and didn't go out with him that day. I guess we'll never know what happened to him."

"Wow. Do you think there could be some truth to that? I mean about the treasure."

"I don't know. Mom thinks it's a crazy idea and the stuff from his boat got carried there on the current. She won't let me go look for anything. I can scuba dive, but it's not a good idea to go by yourself, so I haven't done anything about looking."

"James and I scuba dive. Do you think we could rent some equipment here?"

"Probably. But my mom wouldn't like the idea."

"Maybe we don't have to tell her what we're doing."

Winston shrugged then crumpled up the wrapping papers and tossed them back in the grocery bag. Michel did the same and they went back to work.

It was almost five o'clock when they docked back in Rockport. Winston took most of the lobsters to his buyer and they headed for home, with ten good-sized bugs to cook for dinner.

## Chapter 6
### Off the coast of Damariscove Island

The dark night sky held only a few stars and the moon had not yet risen when an expensive speedboat dropped anchor off the coast of Damariscove Island. The anchor's splash echoed in the still night air. The only other sound was the whispering of waves cresting the rocky shore. Thickening fog made visibility very poor.

"Why do youse think they wants to meet here?" asked Sonny Weather. Sonny's thick New York accent always annoyed his partner Earl Childs. Earl put up with him because Sonny was good for muscle, something often needed in the drug running business.

Earl was a short, skinny white man with thinning black hair, thick black eyebrows and dark eyes that could flash dangerously. He wore a diamond earring stud on one ear. Tonight he wore black wool pants, a crew-neck sweater under a black leather jacket, and he was still cold. Probably because of his short stature, Earl always carried at least one revolver. Nobody was going to take advantage of him without a fight.

Sonny was the product of a pretty Puerto Rican woman and a hulking second generation Russian immigrant. They both thought it was funny to name their son, Sonny Weather. The boy was born after a rousing night of marijuana and booze, which had obviously not totally worn off when they filled out the birth certificate papers in the hospital. After he entered second grade nobody made fun of Sonny's name anymore because he was already as tall as the teacher. Granted, Mrs. Jones was short, but Sonny topped her by a few inches.

Although he was six foot four by the time he made it to tenth grade, Sonny didn't like sports. He was too rough and always caused penalties on the playing field. He wasn't the brightest candle on the cake and he ended up dropping out of school in his junior year. He joined Earl's gang and had more fun intimidating people than conjugating verbs. His broad shoulders and thick muscular arms made short work of anyone Earl told him to 'mess up'.

Sonny loved tattoos. In fact he loved them so much both his arms were covered in bright colored designs. From his wrists to his neck Sonny looked like a copy of the Sunday morning colored comics. His favorite comic book characters wiggled and moved every time he flexed his huge muscled arms. Around his neck he wore a gold chain with a small cross, a gift from his Catholic Puerto Rican mother. She had no idea what Sonny did for a living.

He rubbed at his bald head and the thick white scar that ran past his left eyebrow, a memento of a teenage gang fight. Sonny liked the cold and he wore jeans and a sleeveless t-shirt. Since Earl hadn't answered his question, Sonny asked again. "Why here?"

The deep muffled forlorn sound of a foghorn echoed through the still night air as the fog thickened.

"Probably because this is an uninhabited island close to Boothbay Harbor," said Earl while peering into the foggy darkness. "Wish they'd hurry and show up." He shivered and pulled the jacket closer. He shook his head at Sonny's bare arms. "Aren't you cold?"

"Nah, feels good to me," said Sonny.

The foghorn echoed again.

About that time the sound of a boat engine could barely be heard coming toward them. It suddenly stopped as its lights became visible through the fog. The small fishing boat floated toward them and almost bumped the side of Earl's flashy Glasstream speedboat.

"Hey, watch it youse guys," yelled Sonny.

"Shut up, you idiot," snapped Earl

"Why?" asked Sonny. "Youse said no one lived around here."

Earl gave an exasperated sigh.

A man on the fishing boat dropped a padded bumper between the two boats to prevent any damage to either one before he threw a rope to Sonny. "Hang on to this," he hissed.

Sonny rapped the rope around his arm and easily held the other boat in place.

William Furman, or Will as his friends called him, grabbed the side of Earl's boat and hoisted himself over the side. "Hey, Earl. Glad to see you found the place."

Will wore his brown hair long enough to touch his shoulders. Tonight it was pulled back into a ponytail. He had light brown eyes. He stood five foot nine with a medium build. He wore faded jeans and a collared t-shirt under his wool jacket. He glanced at Sonny's muscled bare arms and moved closer to Earl. Sonny's pale blue-eyed stare made him nervous.

"Yeah, well, let's get this done so I can get out of here," snapped Earl.

Parker Thomas tossed a small duffle bag to Will from the fishing boat. Will unzipped it and held it open while Earl pointed a small flashlight into the opening. The duffle was almost overflowing with stacks of green bills.

"It's all there," said Will. "You want to count it?"

"Nah, I trust you. If it ain't right, I know where you live," snickered Earl.

A little chill ran down Will's back, but he didn't let on. He waited patiently as Earl stowed the duffle and brought out a black canvas bag.

"Here's the stuff," said Earl. "Good quality. You won't find stuff this good on the streets around here."

Will opened the bag and looked at the two large plastic bags inside. Each one contained a pound of white powder. "You already cut the stuff?"

"Only fifty-fifty with aspirin. If you want to change it…"

"Nah, that's good," interrupted Will. He closed the bag and tossed it to Parker. "Nice doing business with ya, Earl." Will climbed back over the edge of the boat onto his own.

Sonny tossed Parker the rope while Will removed the bumper.

Parker watched as the speedboat backed away then sped off. He shivered and looked at Will. "That big guy sure was scary looking."

"Sonny? Oh yeah, he's scary all right. I heard he broke a guy's legs by stomping on them. Nobody wants to mess with Sonny," warned Will.

"Why are we doing business with them?" asked Parker. "What happened to our regular supplier? He run out of cocaine?" Parker snickered.

Will shrugged. "Isn't anybody else left after that big raid by the Coast Guard last winter. Nobody else will come all the way down here from Canada. And Earl's right. No one else has stuff this strong. I'll cut it again before we put it on the street."

While Will stuffed the bag into a storage compartment, Parker started the engine and headed back toward Boothbay Harbor.

Parker Thomas was new to the drug business. When he heard how much money could be made his greedy mind couldn't resist joining up with Will. Parker was barely five foot four, with short spiky blond hair and turquoise blue eyes. His natural disposition was to laziness. Fishing and lobstering were too much work. This seemed so much easier, even if he did have to deal with a guy like Sonny. To him it was worth it.

## Chapter 7
## Maine

    The two weeks sped by as the Ford family visited local sights offered to tourists in the midcoast region of Maine. The puffin museum thrilled Lily and Lacey liked the Farnsworth Art Museum. They ate meal after meal of seafood. Lacey found the lobster rolls to be her favorite and she ate them several times a week; huge chunks of lobster meat on a toasted buttered bun was hard to resist and easier than tackling a whole lobster.

    While the rest of them went sightseeing, Michel spent most of his time out on Winston's boat. He was a fast learner and between the two of them they always finished up early. Michel wasn't as strong as Winston and he often drove the boat while Winston hauled in the traps.

    "I can't believe we only have one more day before we have to head home. Mother said the heat in Arkansas is already wicked this summer," said Lacey lying next to James in bed one morning. "I think I'll miss this little cabin."

    James smiled. It didn't take her long to pick up that adjective. He leaned over and kissed her. "I might have a solution for you," he said. He sat up in bed and picked up his robe. "Mack called me last night. He needs help with a case. What if I went home and all of you stayed for a few more weeks?"

    Lacey looked at him, her mind racing. "You wouldn't mind if we stayed?"

"Of course not. Check today and see if you can rent this cabin for two more weeks." He slid out of bed and put on the robe. "Mack has a missing girl we need to find. Her parents said she ran off to Kansas with her boyfriend. Now she's in some kind of trouble. Anyway, he can pick me up at the airport in Bentonville tomorrow and I can help him with the case."

Lacey hopped out of bed. "I'll get dressed and go talk to the manager about the cabin." She paused looking at the clock. The red numerals glowed 6:30. "Guess I should make every one breakfast first. It's kind of early to bother the manager."

After breakfast Lacey hurried to the manager's house. It was a typical square white saltbox style, but someone had added a front porch. Two rocking chairs and several pots of red geraniums sat to one side of the front door. A tall thin man with a beard answered her knock.

"Hi, Mr. Stuart, I was wondering if we could book our cabin for two more weeks?" she asked. "We'd love to stay longer."

He frowned. "I'm sorry Mrs. Ford but all our cabins are booked up a year in advance. The only way we had one available when your friend called was an unexpected cancellation."

"Oh, of course," said Lacey disappointed. "It's such a lovely place. I can see why it stays full. Can you think of any other place that might have openings?"

He shook his head. "This is the start of our busiest season. I'm sure everybody's booked."

She nodded. "Thanks anyway," she said disappointed.

Annette had arrived and was standing on the porch by the time Lacey walked back to the cabin. "Why the long face?" The breeze from the ocean blew her brown hair into her face and she pushed it back.

"We were hoping to stay longer but everything's booked up," complained Lacey. "James has to head back home for a case, but I could stay with the kids." She led the way inside.

Annette's eyes lit up. "I'm not booked up," she said smiling. "You and Lily could stay in my guest room and Michel could bunk in with Winston. Literally. Winston still has bunk beds in his room. He was planning to move to his own place before Richard went missing. I'm sure he's stayed at home for me. We'd both love to have you stay with us."

Michel walked up behind his mother. "Does this mean we can stay longer?" he asked excitedly. "I really like helping Winston on his boat. He's been paying me to help and I'm saving up for college."

"He shouldn't pay you," objected Lacey.

"Of course he should," said Annette. "Michel's working hard out there on the water."

Lacey shrugged. "They're grown men, I guess they can work out their own solutions."

"Does that mean you'll stay with us?" asked Annette.

"For a while, maybe two weeks," agreed Lacey, smiling.

"You can stay all summer as far as I'm concerned," said Annette cheerfully.

"Wow, could we Mom. I could make a couple of thousand dollars for college," said Michel. "Winston wouldn't mind."

Annette laughed. "He'd love it. He hasn't been able to find anyone else willing to go out with him this summer."

"I couldn't stay that long, but I'll think about letting Michel stay," said Lacey. "If Annette doesn't mind. He eats a lot of food, he'd have to help with the groceries."

"I would, definitely. I'd be happy to help pay for my food," agreed Michel.

"Then it's settled. Tomorrow you can pack up here and come to my house," said Annette. "For now, let's head out to Camden. They've got some great places to shop."

Michel rolled his eyes. "Can you drop me off at the Rockport Harbor? I'd rather go out with Winston."

"Sorry," said Annette. "He's already gone. He left at 5:30 this morning."

"Maybe I'll just hang around here and go to the beach," said Michel. "I don't want to go shopping. I'm sure James doesn't either."

"You're right about that," said James. "I've got a Facetime meeting with Mack in thirty minutes. He's going to fill me in on his case."

"Fine, I guess it's just me and Lily then. She likes to go shopping," said Lacey.

James laughed. "Yes, Dear. You've trained her well."

####

The next morning Lacey drove James down to Portland to catch his early flight home. After packing up their belongings Lacey and the kids headed to Annette's house in Thomaston. The two story wooden frame house was built in the early nineteen hundreds. The Prescott's bought it shortly after they were married. They added a propane heating system and did a lot of rewiring of the antiquated electrical system.

The house was painted white with dark gray trim and a full porch ran across the front. Annette loved gardening and her roses, azaleas and lilacs were in full bloom filling the air with their lovely scents. She rushed out the door as soon as they pulled into the driveway.

"Come on in," she said, picking up one of the suitcases as Michel pulled them from the trunk. "I made lunch."

"You didn't have to do that," objected Lacey.

"Of course I did. I don't get much company and this will be so much fun for me." She opened the front door and led them inside. "It's lonely for me while Winston's gone all day. Working twelve-hour shifts at the hospital means I have four days a week off. Off to be by myself, which isn't very much fun. "

The front of the house was divided into a parlor, dining room, living room and kitchen. Toward the back of the first floor they'd added a laundry room in the old mudroom. The big closet under the stairs had been converted to a small guest bath with toilet and sink. Annette led the way up a set of stairs along the living room wall.

"This first room is Winston's," she said, opening the door. A set of maple bunk beds stood against the far wall, a matching double dresser, desk and chair were the only furniture. A rag rug covered most of the wooden floor space. Winston had tacked posters of his favorite bands and sports heroes on the walls.

"Winston sleeps on the bottom bunk," she told Michel as he carried his suitcase into the room. "He emptied out the right side of the dresser last night for you to use for your clothes."

"Gosh, he didn't have to do that," said Michel.

"He didn't mind," she said.

They left Michel to unpack and walked down the narrow hall to the next door. "This is the guest room."

The bedroom held a wooden four-poster double bed with a homemade patchwork quilt, a matching dresser, nightstand and a rocking chair. Cheery sunflower wallpaper covered three walls and the fourth was painted pale yellow. Another rag rug lay on the wooden floor. A window on the painted wall looked down the hill toward the small harbor on the St. George River. Sunlight sparkled off the flowing water where two fishing boats lay at anchor.

"This is lovely," said Lacey carrying in her suitcase.

"The dresser is empty for you and Lily to use. I know I hate living out of a suitcase; everything gets so wrinkled. My room is at the end of the hall and the bathroom is to the left," she said, stepping toward the door. "It has a shower and an old antique claw-foot tub. Richard remodeled it the year before he went missing."

"You have a lovely home. Thanks so much for inviting us to stay with you," said Lacey.

"Why don't you leave everything until later and let's go eat lunch. Then I thought we could go see the Marshall Point lighthouse and visit Port Clyde," said Annette. "Even Michel might like this trip. The lighthouse is the one used in the movie about *Forrest Gump*, when he ran all the way to Maine. They have a little museum in the lighthouse keeper's house with photos taken while the movie was being filmed. They also have artifacts from when there was a fish cannery nearby. It's only a thirty minute drive from here."

"That sounds interesting," agreed Lacey.

"There's also a beach nearby open to the public. A lot of shiny mica chips are mixed in the beach sand and when he was little Winston called it the 'sparkle beach'," laughed Annette. "One year we found dozens of hermit crabs living there."

"Really?" said Lily. "I want to go. Can we, Mom?"

"We can stop there on the way home and you can play on the beach," said Lacey. "Sounds like you have a wonderful afternoon planned, Annette. Thank you."

## Chapter 8
## Arkansas

James spotted Mack standing behind the airport crowd waiting for the disembarking passengers from his plane. At six foot five Mack's head appeared above most of the onlookers. Mack waved and walked toward him.

"How are you, James? Survived your vacation?" asked Mack, slapping him on the back.

James put down his carry-on and computer bag to hug his friend. They'd worked together at the Bentonville Police Department for years until James was wounded and retired from the force. "You're looking good," commented James.

When Mack's wife Melissa died two years ago after complications from her multiple sclerosis, he had been devastated. Both his sons were grown, married and living in other states. They weren't around to give him much emotional support. When Mack retired from the force and things got worse and he started drinking. James understood how he felt and often dropped by to check on him. Asking Mack to help out on one of his cases had led to a loose partnership between the two men and gave Mack a purpose again.

Mackenzie Stevens bounced back from his depression by taking up jogging and working out at the gym. His broad shoulders and muscular body gave evidence that he spent a lot of time there. His black hair was cut short. He had deep navy blue eyes that grew even darker when he was pissed off, which had cowed a lot of perps he'd arrested. His thick black eyebrows met in the middle of his forehead and Melissa had often teased him about having a uni-brow.

"You hungry?" asked James. "I'm starving. Haven't had more than pretzels all day."

Mack grinned. "You know me, I can always eat. You want BBQ?"

"Sounds great. It's my treat to pay you back for saving me cab fare."

"I never turn down a free meal." Mack laughed. "Let's go to the Rib Crib off Fourteenth Street. I love their four-meat plate." As soon as James' suitcase rolled down the conveyor belt, Mack grabbed it.

Over piled high plates of sliced brisket, pulled pork, ribs and sausage with potato salad and corn on the cob, the men discussed Mack's case.

"The woman's name is Serena Milner. She's twenty-three and a petite little thing with curly blond hair," said Mack.

James laughed. "Everyone looks petite to you, Mack."

"I'm serious here. She's barely five feet tall. I met her once at her parents' house. Don't interrupt," he growled. "Her parents are Joan and Sam Milner. You might remember him from work. He helped out in the coroner's office with paperwork and stuff. Anyway, I've known them for years."

"OK, sorry," said James before taking a bite off a rib bone.

"Serena's engaged to this guy, Tom Blackstone. He's older than her by ten years, a tall skinny guy with brown hair. They met here in town and went to the same church. Her parents said he seemed like a nice enough guy," said Mack, pausing to take a drink of sweet tea. "Tom got laid off at work for Wal-mart in the automotive department. At least that's what he said. I'm beginning to think he got fired."

"Why do you think that?"

"He didn't even look for work around here, just got a job in Kansas City. I talked to one of the guys he worked with at Wal-mart and they said he was suspected of stealing. You know auto parts and stuff. The boss couldn't prove it, but they let him go anyway."

"What makes Serena's parents think she needs help?"

"Boy, you're impatient. I'm getting to that," Mack shook his head.

James grinned and ate his potato salad.

"When Tom moved to Kansas he asked Serena to go with him. They were supposed to get married in a few months anyway, so she went. She called her parents every few days to check in and told them about looking for a job up there and how they were doing. After a month her calls stopped coming. When her mother called Serena, Tom always answered and said she couldn't come to the phone and that she'd call them later."

"But I guess she didn't," interrupted James.

Mack gave him a dirty look. "No, she didn't. Her mother wrote to her, but didn't get any answer to her letters. A few days ago, Serena finally called home in the middle of the night," said Mack before finishing off his brisket. "Serena told her parents that Tom was keeping her a prisoner in their apartment and that he took away her phone. She started crying and said he began hitting her if he didn't like how she cleaned or cooked."

"Crap," said James. "Typical behavior for an abuser. Get the victim away from family and friends then control them."

"I know, what a creep. Anyway she'd managed to find her phone while he was asleep and she begged her parents to come get her. That's when Sam called me and I called you," said Mack. "Between the two of us, I think we can handle getting her home safely."

James grinned. "I'm certain we can."

"We've got a meeting with Sam and Joan Milner tonight at eight. They live not too far from my house. We'll just have time to go by your place and drop off your bags then head over there."

It was a few minutes before eight when Mack pulled up in front of the Milner house. It was a well cared for ranch style with a healthy-looking green, trimmed front lawn and a blooming white dogwood tree in the front yard. Sam waved at them through the big front window as Joan opened the front door.

"Hi, Mackenzie, I'm so glad you're willing to help Serena," said Joan.

"Joan, please call me Mack. Only my mother calls me Mackenzie."

"Ok, Mack. Come on in."

The living room was expansive with a red brick fireplace at one end and two brown leather sofas facing each other in front of it. Framed family photos lined the mantle over the fireplace. Sam sat on the sofa to the left of the fireplace and the men took seats on the one facing him. Sam thanked them for coming.

"Can I get you anything to drink?" asked Joan.

"No thinks, we're fine. Come sit down and we'll talk," said Mack. "This is James Ford. Sam might remember him from years ago when James was a cop in Bentonville." Sam nodded. "James is a licensed private detective now and he specializes in finding and recovering people, among other things. I've worked with him on a few cases."

Joan nodded. "Nice to meet you, Mr. Ford."

James smiled. "Just James will be fine. Tell us about Serena."

The two parents basically told James the same thing he'd heard from Mack. "Now we haven't heard from her in almost a week. We have to get her back home before things get worse," said Joan. She wiped her eyes with a tissue. "We're so worried about her."

Mack reached over and self-consciously patted her arm.

Sam handed Mack a piece of paper. "Here's her address in Kansas. We'll let you handle it from here. I don't even want to know how you'll do it. Just bring my daughter home safe," said Sam. "She's all we have."

## Chapter 9
## Maine

William Furman was trying to figure out the best substance to use to cut this current batch of cocaine. The tiny bit of powder he'd tasted on his fingertip was much stronger than normally sold. He debated between baking soda and more aspirin. The soda was cheaper and those dope heads wouldn't be able to tell it made the stuff kind of fizzy.

Parker Thomas looked at Will. "Whatcha' want me to buy? Aspirin or soda?"

"I'm thinkin'," snarled Will. "I guess the baking soda. Get four big boxes and we'll save whatever we don't use for next time."

Parker nodded.

"Is there any more of that rat poison left?"

Parker grimaced. "Half a box. Who's it for?"

"I think it's time for Belinda to head to heaven to visit her mom."

Parker nodded, but he wasn't happy. "Why do we have to do that to her?"

"Because, nitwit, she's a loose cannon now. She's so far gone if the cops picked her up she'd spill her guts and we'd be done for."

Parker nodded. Will handed him some cash for the baking soda.

"Bring back two of those frozen pizzas, the rising crust kind with all the meat. And a case of beer," ordered Will handing him another forty dollars.

"Right. "

"Do you need to write it down?" asked Will sarcastically.

Parker frowned at him. "I'm not an idiot! I can remember three things."

Will grinned. "Just razzing you, Parker."

"Yeah, well…cut it out." Parker was sensitive about his intelligence. His step-dad always called him 'idiot' before he hit him. Parker had average intelligence; he was just lazy. His grades in school were barely passing, but he did graduate from high school. He figured school was a waste of his time. Besides he was making bundles of cash now and he didn't have to have no college degree to earn it.

While Parker was gone, Will put on a mask and gloves and carefully emptied half of one of the bags of white powder into a container. He gathered his supplies and set them out on the table; a metric scale, dozens of little plastic bags, a small scoop and a wire whisk.

Parker returned with the baking soda and Will carefully mixed two boxes of it into the bowl of cocaine. When he sampled the mix, it tasted about right. Not too salty, just a little fizz and a quick buzz. He began scooping and measuring the mix into the little bags. Each one held a gram of the powdered mix. This one batch would be worth about $40,000 on the street and he figured he could get two batches like this out of each of the big bags. Of course his dealers couldn't sell much of it in the little town of Rockland with only a few dopers here. They fanned out and went to Portland, Bangor, Augusta, and even into New Hampshire and Vermont.

Will picked up two little bags and added a liberal amount of rat poison. He carefully closed the top and sealed it. He used a magic marker to make a green dot on each bag. These two bags would go to Belinda. She was so far gone she'd use them both at once.

After the pizzas were cooked, the men ate in the kitchen and polished off a couple of beers each. Both of them ignored the dirty dishes in the sink. They made enough money to be living in a mansion with full-time cleaning help, but that wasn't a high priority. Most of what they made was spent on women, booze and gambling.

William's house was a nice three-bedroom two-story place with white siding and dark blue trim. The small front porch held a couple of chairs and a porch swing. From the outside, no one would suspect what went on inside. The house sat on two acres of ocean front property. It had its own dock and a boathouse. Will bought it ten years ago in an estate auction. He paid to keep it looking nice outside with a part-time gardener. The inside not so much. He didn't want some housekeeper snooping around.

Will handed Parker a leather pouch with 400 little plastic bags inside. "Only give the dealers fifty bags each. I don't want to flood the market; makes the price go down."

Right now addicts expected to pay $100 per bag. A dealer's cut was 20%. Will and Parker got the rest. They believed selling dope was worth the risk of getting caught.

"What about those bags for Belinda?" asked Parker.

"I'm delivering those myself. Don't want to trust that they might fall into the wrong hands. Can't afford to lose a good customer," joked Will.

Parker left and Will packed away the rest of the mix plus the one he hadn't cut yet. He had a special place in the upstairs bedroom closet even Parker didn't know about. Will didn't trust anyone.

He carried the duffle bag into his bedroom. After stepping around the piles of dirty clothes and girly magazines on the floor, he opened the closet door. Shoving aside the winter coats that hung there, he pushed on the wooden panel at the back. A narrow board opened up to reveal a cubbyhole big enough for the duffle bag and a locked metal box. The box held almost a hundred thousand dollars in cash. Will didn't trust banks either.

He carefully placed the duffle bag on top of the metal box and closed the board. Sliding the coats back in place he stepped back and smiled. Time to go see Belinda.

Belinda Hillman lived in a rundown single story house that had been built by her grandfather ninety years ago. She'd grown up in this house as an only child. Her grandparents and parents were all deceased and she'd inherited the house when her mother died ten years ago.

At fifty-seven Belinda had been divorced twice. Her only son lived in New York and was a lawyer. She hadn't heard from him except for Christmas cards in three years, ever since her drug habit came between them. She started using after her second husband left her for a younger woman, promising herself that she would only take drugs when she had a particularly bad day. But the bad days never seemed to end.

Belinda's full-blown habit caused her to lose her job at the post office after working there for twenty years. Now she lived off SSI, her pension and food stamps.

Belinda's house was in the middle of the woods down a narrow dirt road. Dust flew up behind Will's car as he slowly drove down the road to her rutted, gravel driveway.

Will climbed the rickety front porch steps and knocked on the faded blue front door, peeling chips of paint flecked off onto the torn welcome mat. The whole house was in desperate of repair and a broken rocker sat forlornly beside a dead potted plant on the porch. A cracked front window was covered with cardboard and duct tape.

Belinda opened the door to Will in a faded, dirty, torn housedress. Her brown hair was unwashed and straggled down to her shoulders in greasy curls. Her watery blue eyes were red rimmed with dark circles around them. She grinned and brushed a curl off her cheek. "Hi, Will."

She motioned for Will to come inside, but the stench of rotten food and her unwashed body kept him on the sagging wooden porch.

"I know your stuff is a little late this week," murmured Will. "So there's no charge."

Belinda grinned. "Thanks Will. I won't forget this," she said grabbing the envelopes. "You want something to drink?"

"Nah, got to make other deliveries," said Will. She didn't know he never delivered the stuff himself unless it was an occasion like this.

"OK, thanks." She quickly shut the door behind her, eager to get her next high.

Will heard her lock the door and he shook his head. No one in his right mind would try to rob this falling down wreck of a place.

He whistled a little tune as he walked back to his black Cadillac. He grimaced at the dust all over the normally shiny paint. He'd have to go by the car wash.

## Chapter 10

Winston wiped the sweat off his forehead that was threatening to get in his eyes. Even with Michel's help it was turning into a long day. He looked at the almost overflowing lobster tank and grinned. It was an exceptionally good haul. He was only half way through the summer season and he'd already made enough money to see him through the winter. Maybe he could go full-time to college since he wouldn't have to get a winter job this year.

"How many traps are left?" asked Michel glancing back at Winston. Today he was steering the boat as Winston insisted on pulling the traps himself. The traps were so laden with lobsters they were almost too heavy for Michel to haul out of the water. Winston figured to save time by doing it himself.

"Only ten more then we can head home."

"Great." Michel knew the route by now and he headed to the next trap site.

While they measured the last of the catch, Michel asked, "How far from here is that place your dad went missing?"

Winston looked up and frowned. "Damariscove Island is down by Boothbay Harbor. It's about forty miles on the water."

"Oh, that's pretty far. I thought maybe we could go by it today."

"It would take over two hours to get there," said Winston. "Maybe we could go tomorrow if we started early enough."

"You said your dad was interested in some kind of treasure. Is there supposed to be something buried on Damariscove Island?"

"It's a tall tale some old timers tell," said Winston putting the last lobster into the tank. "Personally I think it's a bunch of bull, just some old myth."

"But how did it get started?" hollered Michel over the engine's roar as he turned the boat back toward Rockport Harbor. It would be time for supper by the time they got back. Annette was making fried chicken tonight and his mouth watered thinking about it.

Winston walked into the cabin and leaned against the wall. It was hard to talk over the noise of the boat motor and the waves they stirred up.

"There was some pirate way back in the 1600's who traveled along the coast around here. He probably wasn't the only one but his legend lived longer than any other one. Seems he burned down a town and stole all kinds of 'booty' for a while," said Winston. "They called him the Dread Pirate Dixce."

Michel laughed, "Doesn't seem like a pirate named Dixie would be very scary."

"Depends on which side of the cannon you're facing," said Winston.

"True. So he hid some of his treasure on the island?"

"Some say Damariscove and some say Cushings Island. Anyway, people have been hunting for it for hundreds of years," said Winston. "I've never heard of anyone finding any treasure."

"But your dad thought it was real?"

Winston shrugged. "I don't know how serious he was, but he talked about it. He said the water levels have changed a lot over the past four hundred years. He thought the islands would have been bigger back then, so maybe the treasure was now under water."

"Huh, that's interesting."

"We sometimes went scuba diving around both those islands. We never found any treasure but the scenery is great underwater. And there are shipwrecks in several places off the coast that we're allowed to explore."

Michel pulled up to the dock and Winston jumped off the boat to tie it up. They unloaded the catch and put the tank in the back of the pickup bed. It took both of them to lift it.

They got in the truck and Winston looked at Michel. "Dad said he might go diving after checking the pots that day. I guess he had some kind of accident." He sighed. "If I'd been with him it might not have happened. He might still be alive."

The look on Winston's face made Michel stop asking questions. "You can't blame yourself. Something could have happened to you that day, too. That would've been awful for your mother."

Winston shrugged and started the truck. "I know, but sometimes I still feel bad."

## Chapter 11
## Arkansas

    Mack and James left early the next morning to go get Serena Milner. Since they didn't know how Tom would react, they were both armed. James carried his S&W Bodyguard 380 Crimson Trace revolver. Mack favored his Springfield Armory HELLCAT 9mm semi-automatic pistol, which held eleven rounds of ammunition. Both men knew how dangerous a retrieval could be and they wore bulletproof vests under their shirts.

    They headed north on Interstate 49 to Missouri. After three hours of driving they left the Interstate for Route 66 through Joplin into Kansas. After passing through Galena they drove another fifteen minutes before they spotted a sign for **Nelson's Old Riverton Store**.

    "Hey, it says they serve food," noted James. "Should we stop for lunch?"

    "Might as well," agreed Mack. "If Tom leaves work to go home for lunch we don't want to meet him. I'd rather find Serena alone."

    James parked his SUV in front of the store. They ate their burgers slowly then perused the store shelves until one o'clock.

    Back in the car James studied the GPS. "We're only ten minutes from the house. How do you want to handle this?"

    "You have more experience at this than I do," said Mack.

    James shrugged. "It's your case."

    "I'll defer to your vast experience," joked Mack.

    "Fine." James drove through Riverton toward the house on Bluebird Lane. He parked on the street two houses away. "Let's circle the house first in case Tom's home."

The small white two-bedroom single story house stood back from the street surrounded by tall trees. Several thick azalea bushes with pink flowers blooming edged up against the front walls. A tiny porch held one plastic lawn chair. There was no vehicle in the driveway.

The neighborhood was quiet and no one was on the street.

"He could have parked in the garage," said James. "I'll check that small window on the side of the garage and you scout around the back of the house."

Mack nodded and slipped away between the trees.

The garage was empty when James peered through the window. Mack came up beside him. "No one in the backyard. Kitchen and one bedroom were clear. The blinds to the second bedroom were closed tight," whispered Mack. "I couldn't see inside that room."

"That's probably where he keeps her locked up when he's gone."

"Makes sense, the master bedroom probably has a bathroom attached," agreed Mack. "So what's the plan?"

"Let's go around back and knock on the window. Maybe she'll open the blinds," said James. "He's probably secured the window, but maybe we can break in."

Mack shook his head. "There are makeshift bars on that window."

James grimaced. "OK, we'll go in the back door."

They hurried around to the back door. James used the butt of his gun to break a small window on the door. After knocking away any glass shards, he reached in carefully and unlocked the door. They stepped into the kitchen. It was spotless; clean dishes drying in the dish rack, all the counters wiped clean. The trashcan by the door was empty with a new plastic bag lining the inside. A small table with only two chairs had flowered placemats and silverware on it ready for the next meal.

They walked into the living room. It was neat and orderly as well. The sofa had flowered pillows in place with end tables and lamps at each end. The old shag carpet showed signs of being newly vacuumed and magazines were stacked neatly on a coffee table.

"Looks like he keeps her on a short leash. Everything is spotless," observed Mack.

They walked down the hall to the master bedroom. There was a shiny new deadbolt lock on the outside of the door.

Mack shook his head in disgust. "She'd be trapped if a fire started in this place."

James knocked on the door and called her name. "Serena, you in there?"

They heard her walk to the door. "Who are you?" she asked in a frightened voice.

"Your parents sent us to bring you home," said Mack. "I'm going to unlock the door, so don't be frightened."

She stepped back. "OK. I'm out of the way."

The lock clicked as Mack slid back the bolt. He pushed on the door and opened it wide. Serena stood with her arms wrapped around her thin body. A huge purple bruise stood out against the pale skin on her cheek. Tears ran down her face. She wore a pair of jeans, a blue t-shirt and leather sandals. Her brown hair was pulled back into a loose ponytail.

"Thank you," she mumbled. "I don't think I would have lasted much longer." She started shaking and collapsed onto the bed. "I thought he was going to kill me last night." She put her hands to her face and began sobbing.

Mack stood back, not sure what to do for the crying young woman. Finally he stepped toward her and patted her shoulder. "Let's get your things and take you home."

Serena flung herself toward him and huddled against his chest. "I'm so scared. What if he comes back?"

Mack put his arms around her and patted her back. "Shh, we'll take care of you. Where's your suitcase?"

She pointed under the bed.

James grabbed two suitcases out from under the bed while Mack comforted Serena. He put them on the bed and opened them both.

"One of those is Tom's," she said wiping her eyes with the back of her hand.

"Doesn't matter," said James. "Let's fill them both."

She nodded and moved toward the closet. Mack helped her grab her shirts and a few dresses hanging in there. While James quickly folded the items, Serena showed Mack which dresser drawers held her jeans and under clothes.

"I'll get my things from the bathroom," she said. Five minutes later she came out with a stuffed makeup bag. "That's all of it."

"Anything you want from the rest of the house?" asked James.

"Not a thing." She looked less frightened. "I just want out of here."

The three of them made it to the living room when they heard the key turn in the front door. Tom stepped inside. He took one look at the suitcases and Serena.

"What the hell's going on here?" he yelled rushing toward her.

Mack stepped in front of Serena. "We're taking her home."

"Like hell you are!" Tom grabbed a pistol from the back of the waistband on his pants. "She's my fiancée. She's not going anywhere!" He pointed the gun at Mack.

James dropped both suitcases and whipped out his revolver. "Drop it, Tom! No one needs to get hurt today."

Tom swiveled the gun toward James and fired. The bullet slammed into the wall behind James' head as he ducked and fired his weapon. Tom had dropped to his knees causing James' bullet to miss him. It hit the front door frame with a loud thud.

Serena screamed. Mack pushed her into the hallway and he pulled out his gun.

"This is pointed at your chest, Tom! Drop your weapon!" hollered Mack.

Instead Tom flung himself behind the sofa and fired at Serena. "You bitch!" he screamed. Bullets hit the walls and ceiling as the smell of gunpowder filled the air.

Mack fired his weapon into the sofa causing tufts of stuffing to fly through the air. James grabbed Serena by the arm and pulled her into the kitchen. "Go out the back door!" he ordered.

Her eyes wide with terror, Serena ran across the room toward the door and rushed outside into the back yard.

Tom slid to the edge of the sofa and fired at Mack missing him completely. It was obvious he was a poor shot and Mack ducked back into the hallway and waited until Tom ran out of bullets. When he heard the clicks of the empty pistol and an angry curse from Tom, he stepped back into the living room.

"Come out and put your hands up where I can see them," yelled Mack.

Instead Tom charged out from behind the sofa and ran toward Mack with a knife. He waved the knife wildly as he rushed forward.

Mack rolled his eyes and calmly fired a bullet into Tom's hand. The knife dropped to the floor as blood spurted from Tom's palm.

"You shot me!" screamed Tom cursing. Suddenly he sat down on the floor and started crying as blood dripped down his fingers. "My hand's broken," he sobbed clutching it to his chest. "You'll pay for this."

James dialed 911 and as he explained what happened to the police, Serena came back inside through the front door.

Calmly walking up to Tom, she drew back her hand and slapped him hard across the face. His head flew back and he looked up at her in shock.

Tom bellowed, "Why'd you do that, honey?"

"Pay back's a bitch," said Serena through gritted teeth. "And don't call me honey. In fact don't ever call me anything." She tore off her engagement ring and dropped it in his lap. "I don't ever want to see you again!"

She walked over to Mack, grinning. "That felt good."

Tom blubbered on the floor and cradled his wounded hand. "I'm sorry. Serena, honey, I'll never hit you again, I promise. Please don't leave me," he begged. "I can't live without you. I'll die if you leave."

Mack watched her face to see if she would fall for Tom's lies. He's seen so many women do that, and go right back into an abusive relationship.

But Serena's expression hardened. "Don't even go there, Tom. I don't believe a word you say. You've burned your bridges with me. You're a liar and I have the bruises to prove it."

James finished his call and sirens could already be heard heading their way. He grabbed a wad of paper towels from the kitchen and carried them over to the still crying Tom.

"Here, use these. Wrap them around the wound. Don't worry, you're not going to bleed to death," he said coldly. "There's an ambulance on the way."

A police car roared into the driveway and screeched to a halt. Two uniformed officers rushed to the door with weapons drawn. Mack and James had already holstered their revolvers and were ready with their 'license to carry' cards.

EMT's rushed in and began working on Tom as a second police car arrived.

The officers lowered their guns and proceeded questioning everyone.

Mack was proud of Serena as she bravely told her side of the story. After an hour of questioning everyone involved, the police let Mack take Serena and her suitcases to James' car. Tom was taken to the local hospital under guard.

James followed the officers' vehicle to the police station where they all signed statements and were allowed to leave. It was after four o'clock when they started toward Arkansas.

"Thank you so much for helping me," said Serena from the backseat. "Could I ask one more favor? Can we stop to get something to eat?"

"Sure, no problem," said James. ""What do you want?"

"Anything. Tom limited my food," she explained. "He said I was getting fat so he only allowed me to eat yogurt and fruit for weeks."

"That's horrible. I'm so sorry," said Mack.

"It's my own fault for getting mixed up with him."

"Hey, it's not your fault. He was a liar and an abuser. Abusers are great at conning women," said James. "So what do you really want to eat?"

She grinned. "A big steak with French fries with a chocolate milkshake."

"I think we can handle that," said Mack.

After stopping at a Denny's for dinner, the men watched in amazement as the tiny woman ate her way through a t-bone steak and a huge pile of fries. They finished their own meal before she was half way through hers.

"That was so good," she said as they were leaving. "Thanks, I'll pay you back."

James smiled. "No problem. It's part of the service."

After getting gas they drove back to Arkansas. It was almost midnight but Serena had phoned her parents and they were waiting up.

They rushed to the porch when James pulled into the driveway.

It was a teary reunion and even Mack felt his throat get tight with emotion.

## Chapter 12
## Maine

Annette was busy in the kitchen making breakfast when Lacey walked in. She was already dressed in a blouse and shorts.

"Good morning," said Lacey. "Something smells good."

"I'm making waffles," said Annette quietly.

When she turned around Lacey noticed that her eyes were red-rimmed as if she had been crying. Lacey took a step closer. "Annette, is something wrong?"

Annette's lower lip quivered and she nodded. "Today is the anniversary of when Richard went missing." She wiped a tear off her cheek with the hem of her apron.

Lacey quickly wrapped her arms around Annette's shoulders and hugged her. "Do you want us to leave so you can be alone?"

"Oh, no," mumbled Annette. "That would be worse. I need company and distractions until this awful day is over."

"All right." Lacey patted her back. "Let me finish the waffles for you."

Annette sniffed and nodded. "I'll put the butter and syrup on the table."

The microwave beeped and Lacey took the tray of bacon out of it. Then she removed a waffle from the waffle maker and put it on top of the stack on a plate in the oven where they were keeping warm. She sprayed oil on the waffle grill and poured the last of the batter.

"This is the last waffle," she told Annette. "The batter's gone."

Annette poured herself a cup of coffee and sat down at the table. "I'll be alright in a minute," she said softly. She blew her nose on a tissue and took a sip of coffee.

Just as the last waffle finished cooking, Winston, Michel and Lily came into the kitchen and hurriedly sat down at the table. "Oh boy, waffles!" said Lily when she saw the piled high plate her mother carried to the table.

"There are sliced strawberries in a bowl in the refrigerator," Annette told Winston. "Would you get those and the milk?"

Winston nodded. He remembered what the day signified, too. He noticed his mother's reddened eyes and gave her a little hug before going to open the refrigerator.

They all made quick work of breakfast and the happy chatter of the children was soothing to Annette. She smiled when Lacey wiped syrup off Lily's chin.

"Winston, what are your plans for today?" Annette asked.

He shrugged. "We pulled all the traps yesterday so I can do whatever you want to do. It won't hurt to let them sit until tomorrow."

Annette smiled. "I'd like to go to Damariscove Island and drop a few flowers on the sight where they found your dad's equipment floating. It's not like there's a grave to go to..."

"Sure, Mom. We can do that. I fueled up the boat yesterday and it's not that far."

Annette looked at Lily. "Would you like to go out on Winston's boat?"

Lily's eyes widened. "Yeah! I've been wanting to go out, but he's always working and Michel said I'd get in the way."

"Hey, I didn't say it that way," protested Michel. "I just thought you'd get bored. All we do is pull traps all day."

Annette laughed. "I'm sure he had your best interest at heart, Lily. It is pretty boring watching them pull traps for hours. But the weather is beautiful today and it will be fun to go out," she said. "You need to take a sweater or sweatshirt because even though it's warm on land, it gets chilly out on the water."

"I have a sweatshirt," said Lily. "I'll go get it."

"Why don't we make sandwiches and have a picnic lunch, too," suggested Lacey.

"That's a great idea. Richard loved picnics. We'll go ashore for a lunch break," said Annette. "Do they still let people go on to the island?" she asked Winston.

"Yes. They have a caretaker on that island during the summer. He stays in the old Life Saving Station and there's even a little museum," said Winston getting excited. "There are hiking trails and it's really pretty out there."

"It sounds like a lot of fun," said Lacey. She began gathering up the breakfast dishes.

After making sandwiches and filling a picnic basket with cookies, chips and apples, Annette loaded everyone into her SUV. On the way to the Rockport Harbor she stopped and bought flowers. They parked in the small lot at the harbor and Winston led the way to his boat. He helped the women and Lily climb on board then Michel released the ropes attached to the pier. The strong smell of saltwater hung in the air. Seagulls flew overhead squawking.

The birds fascinated Lily. "Look at that really big one," she said, pointing to a particularly large gull.

Michel hopped on board as Winston started the engine. Michel dug out life vests while Winston maneuvered out of the harbor around the other boats anchored offshore.

"I think this one is small enough for you," he told Lily as he pulled the smallest orange vest out of the locker.

"It should work for her," said Annette. "It was Winston's when he was about eight."

"But I'm older than eight," protested Lily.

Annette laughed. "That's true. But Winston was as big as you are now when he was eight. So it will work just fine."

Michel helped Lily adjust the straps and buckles while Annette and Lacey put on vests.

The boat sped up as they left the harbor. The sun sparkled on the deep blue water and the seagulls followed them for several miles, much to Lily's enjoyment. They passed several lobstermen who waved as they sped by. A pod of dolphins swam by as they turned south.

Winston pointed them out to Lily. She watched enthralled as they passed.

They reached the island by twelve-thirty. Winston moored the boat with ease and after removing their vests they all clamored onto the wooden dock and waited while he tied ropes to metal cleats embedded on the wood.

They walked along the shore enjoying the sight of sea birds overhead. Several black and white terns swooped and dived in the updraft currents, their noisy calls filling the air. Winston pointed out their nesting sites on the rocks. No trees blocked the view of the entire island.

"Terns nest on the ground in weeds and rocks," explained Winston. Then he pointed to a large pelican at the water's edge.

"Wow, look how big his beak is," said Lily as the bird scooped up fish from the water.

They walked along a dirt path to a small building. Inside the museum the caretaker gave them a little of the history of the island. The caretaker this year was a grizzled retired fisherman with gray hair and beard. His bright blue eyes lit up when he talked.

"This island was first settled by Native American Abenaki Indians." He looked at Lily and winked. "You might even find an arrowhead if you look hard enough. The entire island is only half a mile wide and two miles long. By 1604 some European explorers found the island and started a fishing colony here. But the colony suffered from disease and the weather that first year. And the Indians weren't happy with the settlers invading their land and they sometimes attacked them."

Lily listened intently.

He continued. "By the 1800's there was a pretty good-sized fishing village and some of the settlers farmed and grazed animals here. The ice from the island pond was stored for summer use and they even found granite and started a small quarry. In 1896 the Life Saving Station was built on the south end of the island. Rescuers were frequently needed to save shipwrecked sailors."

Lily's mouth dropped open. "There were shipwrecks?"

"Sure were, little Miss. Some wicked ones," he said nodding. "The Coast Guard took over in 1959 and closed the station here when their services moved to Boothbay. This island is owned by the Boothbay Region Land Trust now and no one lives here anymore."

"But you're here," pointed out Lily.

He laughed. "Only in the summer so I can help the tourists and make sure no one does anything to harm the birds out here. We have lots of trails and you folks feel free to walk around. Just make sure you don't leave any trash behind when you go," he admonished.

"Thank you so much for the information," said Lacey as she guided Lily to the door.

After leaving the museum they walked along a trail listening to the surf roll over the granite beaches. When they found several big flat rocks, they used one for a table and spread out their picnic lunch. Two seagulls landed nearby hoping for picnic leftovers. When they finished eating Lily threw pieces of bread to them. One of the birds didn't even wait for the bread to hit the ground but grabbed it midair, much to Lily's delight.

Lacey snapped a few photos on her phone to show to James later. After cleaning up their trash and stowing it back in the basket, they headed back to the boat. Lacey took a few photos of the beach, the birds and the museum as she walked back.

After getting settled back on the boat, Winston headed to the east side of the island. When they reached the approximate spot where the coast guard found his father's floating debris Annette began tossing daisies into the water.

"Miss Annette, can I throw some flowers?" asked Lily. "The blue ones?"

Annette handed her the blue *for-get-me-not's* and Lily reverently tossed them overboard. Winston waited for his mother to nod to him then he turned the boat around and headed for open water. It was close to six o'clock by the time they docked and drove home. Everyone voted on bowls of cereal for dinner. Lily was so tired she went to bed as soon as she finished eating.

"I'm so sorry about Richard," Lacey told Annette as she dried the bowls.

Annette nodded. "I just wish they'd found his body so I could bring him home."

## Chapter 13

Monday morning when Winston and Michel went out to pull the lobster traps it was drizzling rain. Besides the overalls they wore bright yellow waterproof raincoats with hoods. Even with the coats, they were soaked and miserable by midmorning. In fact it was turning into a miserable day all the way around when they found only a few lobsters in the traps. In fact a few traps had no lobsters at all even though the bait was eaten.

Michel dumped a baby grouper fish over the side of the boat. "Could the fish have eaten all the bait and scared off the lobsters?" asked Michel.

Winston shook his head. "Looks like someone stole my catch in this area," he said as he was refilling bait bags.

"Does this happen often?" asked Michel, stuffing bait into another bag and tying it inside the empty trap.

"No, not often. If you get caught taking someone else's catch there's a big fine and if it happens again you could lose your license." Winston sighed and looked out across the water.

"I can't believe someone took your lobsters," he said. When Winston threw his trap back into the water Michel drove the boat to the next area. He could see Winston was upset. "It sucks that someone stole them."

"It isn't that actually. I've been thinking about my dad. Ever since we went to Damariscove Island it's been bothering me," Winston admitted. "I wish I could go diving out there to see if I could find something, anything the Coast Guard might have missed."

"Do you scuba dive?" asked Michel.

"Yes, Dad and I used to go spear fishing. I haven't been since…you know. I can't go out alone, it's too dangerous. If anything happened to me I don't know what my Mom would do."

Michel stopped the boat beside more of Winston's floats. When the sound of the engine died down he turned to Winston. "I dive," said Michel excitedly.

Winston turned and looked at him. "You do?"

"Sure, me, my dad and step-brother have gone out several times. We mostly go in Beaver Lake, but once we went diving off the coast of Galveston Island in Texas."

Winston nodded and looked thoughtful.

They hurriedly worked the line of traps. Luckily these held several lobsters each.

Finally Winston told him, "I still have most of our dive equipment. We'd have to check it all over and fill the tanks, but it's top of the line stuff my dad bought. I have four tanks and extra flippers. The water temperature up here is always in the fifties and we have to wear dry-suits. It feels pretty darn cold after a few minutes. I think my dad's extra suit will fit you," Winston told Michel. "Do you think your mom would let you dive with me?"

"I don't know. I always go with my dad," said Michel, frowning.

"Is he coming back to Maine when he finishes the case back home?" asked Winston, steering the boat to his next set of traps.

"I'll ask my mom tonight, she'll know," said Michel. "We could present this like another 'missing person' case to him. What do you think?"

Winston grinned for the first time that day. "Great idea. I could offer to pay him so it would be a legitimate case."

When they got home that evening Michel was surprised to find James at the house.

"So you found the girl in Kansas?" he asked sitting down across from his stepfather.

James grinned and nodded. "We did."

"Are you staying in Maine for a while now?"

"Unless Mack calls again." James looked at Michel. He could sense something was up. "Do you have something else you want to ask me?"

Michel looked at Winston who nodded for him to ask. "Winston wondered if he could have our help on a missing person case."

James looked at Winston. "To find your father?"

Winton nodded. "I know it's a long shot. The Coast Guard couldn't even find his boat, but I wanted to do some diving off Damariscove Island where the debris was found. I could pay for your help."

Annette looked at Winston. "Oh, honey, I don't know if that's a good idea." She walked over and hugged him. "I'd hate for you to be disappointed."

Winston hugged her back and looked in her eyes. "I need to do this, Mom. I might find nothing, but I want to look."

She gave him a squeeze and nodded, then looked at James. "What do you think?"

"I'm willing. Michel and I know how to dive. But I insist on doing this as a friend. No fee. In exchange for letting us stay with you," said James.

Winston grinned. "All right. I'll check out the equipment I've got in the garage tonight. We can rent anything else we need from the *Frogdogz* dive shop in Rockland."

####

Over the next few days Winston made certain the tanks and equipment he had were in good working order. One evening he and Michel took the tanks to be filled with the oxygen mixture after they finished pulling traps. Richard's second older dry-suit fit Michel but James needed to rent a suit, swim fins and face mask.

On Thursday they went to *Frogdogz* to rent what James needed. The shop was off Main Street down toward the harbor.

"My friend David Pearson and his father Chris own this place," said Winston pulling his truck up to the front of the shop. "They sometimes volunteer with the 'search and rescue' team. They went out with the police last year when a party barge sank off the coast of Deer Isle."

A bell dinged as they opened the front door to the store. Chris stood behind the counter while David was restocking facemasks. Chris wore wire-rim glasses and kept his head shaved. His neatly trimmed beard was white with a touch of gray. He looked up when they entered.

"Hi, Winston," welcomed Chris. "What can I help you with today?"

"These are my relatives from Arkansas," said Winston. "My cousin Michel and his dad, James. We want to dive off Damariscove Island and James needs to rent some gear including a dry-suit."

Chris smiled. "Nice to meet you. We used to live in Bentonville. When the weather got to be too hot down south, we moved up here." He shook hands with James. "David can help get you a suit. He's better at sizing people than I am."

David walked over and looked James up and down. "Probably a size 'large' will work." David stood a few inches taller than James. With broad shoulders, brown hair and trimmed beard he was ruggedly handsome. His pale blue eyes sparkled with mischief. He and Winston had gotten into their share of trouble as teenagers. David was never shy about instigating a prank or two. Winston had been a little jealous of all the girls David attracted.

"Nice to see you again Winston. How's the lobstering going?"

"It's harder without Dad's help, but Michel's worked with me this summer so I'm having a good year," said Winston. "How are Samantha and Carolyn?"

"Sam's working at Camden Bank and Mom enjoys staying home and sewing crafts."

"Tell Carolyn I miss her candy. Will she be making any this Christmas?" asked Winston.

"She's already planning it. I'll let her know you're interested. So let's see if I'm right about your size," said David leading James to a rack of dry-suits.

James got everything he needed at *Frogdogz*. He was impressed with their inventory and ended up buying himself a new mask.

"This one fits better than the one I have back home," he explained to Lacey when they got back to the house. She just rolled her eyes at him.

"Boys and their toys," she laughed. "At least it's not a motorcycle."

"Hmmm," said James thoughtfully. "I saw a great *Harley* on sale back home."

"Don't even think about it," she warned.

That night they watched the weather report and determined that the next day would be perfect for diving; sunny, clear and as warm as it ever got in Maine.

Winston could barely contain his excitement. Finally he could see for himself if there were any clues that had been missed that might explain what happened to his father.

## Chapter 14
### Off the coast of Damariscove Island

They left Thomaston the next morning before four o'clock and the sun was just coming up as the *Chelsea Two* pulled out of Rockport Harbor. Lacey went with them as they felt it would be safer to have someone stay on the boat while they dived. She'd gone out with James several times in the past. Winston showed her where the first aid kit was kept and how to use the boat's radio in case she needed to call for help from the Coast Guard.

By the time they reached Damariscove Island the sun was high and shining brightly off the blue water. There were no tourists on the island this morning. They saw the caretaker sitting in front of the museum smoking a pipe. He waved as their boat passed and circled the island to the east side where Richard's boat debris had been floating.

Winston stopped the boat about forty yards from shore and Michel dropped the anchor.

"So when the Coast Guard looked for your dad, what did they actually find?" asked James as he pulled on his dry-suit. Lacey zipped the back and he sat down to put on the swim fins. He tugged them into place and looked over at Winston.

"All they found was his life vest, a small deck chair and some float pillows. The pillows had *Chelsea* sewn on them. They were a present from my mom," said Winston. "They never found his boat and assumed it had floated out to sea. They searched a one hundred mile radius but never found anything else."

James nodded. "So what was the weather like that day?"

"It was stormy in the afternoon but cleared off. I hate that I wasn't with him. I started out that morning feeling sick, but later felt better and ended up going camping with some friends. We were out of cell phone tower range and I didn't even know he was missing until I came home the next day." Winston shook his head. "Dad told Mom that he was going to do a little diving after he pulled his traps. We're assuming he had an accident, but then his boat should have been found anchored somewhere."

"And he didn't have any lobster traps around this island?"

Winston shook his head. "No, this is way out of our area. I think he was exploring for pirate treasure."

Lacey looked surprised. "Pirate treasure? In Maine? I thought pirates hung around warmer waters like the Caribbean."

"We had some, too," explained Winston. "There are plenty of legends about pirate treasure here. During the sixteen and seventeen hundreds boats and towns sometimes got raided by pirates. Dad was interested in a pirate named Dixce Bull. Legend has it that he was the first real pirate this far up north. He only raided for a year or so but he burned down a settlement and that earned a ransom on his head."

"Huh, and he hid treasure on Damariscove Island?" asked Lacey.

"That's one legend. My dad said the ocean water was lower back then and that made the islands bigger. He thought the treasure had never been found because now it was under water." Winston pulled on his fins.

"But no one knows what actually happened that day?" asked Lacey.

"The Coast Guard divers didn't find any signs of dad's boat being wrecked but I'd still like to see what's down there," he said nodding toward the water.

Several white seagulls flew overhead watching to see if the boat would supply them with a meal. Their loud calls filled the air while they circled the boat. After a few minutes they left.

When the three men were dressed and ready they took turns dropping into the water. "Be careful!" she called to James. He saluted her and ducked his head under the water.

She adjusted her sunglasses against the sun's glare on the water and watched their shadows disappear as they swam deeper. She sighed then pulled a deck chair into the shade of the cabin and got out a book to read.

Visibility was limited in the cold water for the divers. Silt made it worse if a fin happened to bump the bottom. Winston turned on his underwater flashlight and led the way toward the island shoreline.

They swam over a rocky area and Michel spotted a big lobster eating something. A school of fish swam so close several brushed his arm as they passed. He spotted a lone seal off to his left with gray fur and white spots. Curious, the seal approached him then swam away.

Michel followed Winston and James followed him. Near the shoreline the current pulled at them making swimming more difficult. After a few minutes the tide settled down and it became easier to avoid bumping into sharp rocks. They scoured the rocky edges of the island for thirty minutes before Winston spotted something and waved them over.

Almost buried in waving sea grass and kelp was a blue swim fin. Winston pulled it out causing silt to float up obscuring their vision. They waited for the water to clear and he held up the fin for them to see. Faintly painted on the bottom of the rubber sole of the fin was the word *Chelsea*. They pushed aside kelp and weeds but only found a few aluminum cans and bits of broken fishing floats.

Michel picked up the trash and put it in the mesh bag attached to his weight belt. Humans are so trashy he thought. Some people treated the ocean like a personal garbage can.

Winston swam further ahead and disturbed a large green crab that scooted away. He pulled at the sea kelp and brushed his hands over crevasses in the rocks. Several shrimp scurried away but he didn't find anything of his dad's. After another thirty minutes of looking he turned around and headed back to the boat with the others following him.

Lacey helped the men climb back on board the boat. They quickly removed their masks and stored the oxygen tanks. Winston was examining the fin when James came up beside him. There were a few small barnacles attached to it and some green scum that Winston wiped off with a rag. "This is definitely my dad's," said Winston. "My mom painted the boat name on the bottom. She does that to all of them, in case they get mixed up with someone else's." He lifted his foot and showed them the name on the bottom of his fin. *Chelsea Two* stood out in white painted letters.

James reached out and took the fin from Winston. He examined it closely. The rubber was completely intact except for one small round hole. There were no cracks or broken off bits. James put his finger into the whole to get an idea of its size then he looked at Winston.

"What do you suppose made that?" asked Winston, looking at the hole.

"It looks suspiciously like a bullet hole," said James.

Lacey and Michel hurried over to see the swim fin.

"Are you sure?" asked Michel.

James nodded. "It's too perfectly round. I think it was made by a twenty-two."

Winston's eyes widened. "Someone shot at my dad?"

"It looks like it."

"We need to tell the police," said Michel.

"As soon as we get back, I'll go with Winston to the police station," said James.

Winston was shaken. "Does this mean someone may have murdered my father?"

"It could be," said James solemnly.

Shaken at the thought, Winston sat down hard on the deck. After a minute he pulled off his swim fins and dry-suit. "Michel, pull the anchor, please. We're heading home."

They were a somber group as the long trip home gave them plenty of time to think about what might have happened to Richard Prescott.

## Chapter 15
## Maine

Office Dayes parked her car in the lot beside the Rockland Police Department. Walking toward the beige brick building, she scanned the area and noted the fishing boats still anchored in the harbor. The building had a great view of the harbor from the second story windows. Unfortunately her desk was on the first level sandwiched between two other desks. But every chance she got she ate lunch outside and enjoyed the view. After straightening her uniform, she opened the door to the building.

Glory Dayes graduated from the Maine Criminal Justice Academy three years ago. Six months ago she finished training and joined the Maine Marine Underwater Crime Scene Team. She'd learned scuba diving from her father by the time she was twelve years old. Now she could enjoy diving while investigating underwater crime scenes. Of course there was a lot more involved than enjoying the swim. She learned how to document a crime scene and she was part of the search and rescue dive team for underwater accidents and deaths.

She walked under the columned entry into the building and headed to her desk.

"Morning, Glory Dayes," snickered Officer Adams.

He loved to tease her about her name. Why her parents named her *Glory Dayes* was beyond her. She'd gotten plenty of teasing all through school.

"Morning, Devon," she said. Officer Adam Adams was a good cop, and she figured he only teased her because he'd probably been teased himself growing up. That was why he preferred to go by his middle name of Devon.

Glory sat down at her desk and while her computer booted up she searched a drawer for an elastic band. She pulled her long curly black hair back into a ponytail. When the computer was ready she pulled up a program to search for any new crimes that occurred in the three days she'd been off duty. Her dark violet eyes scanned the screen. There was nothing of note until she saw that the police had found a woman's body. She pulled up the description of the case.

A man had been bird watching in the woods when his dog ran off to a lone house and began barking and scratching at the back door. When the birdwatcher approached the house he noted a foul odor and he called the police. Inside was the decomposing body of a woman identified as Belinda Hillman. Because her fingerprints were on file, she was quickly identified by her rap sheet for drug possession and prostitution.

Glory pulled up the coroner's report. What first appeared as a simple drug overdose was ruled poisoning. The cocaine Belinda snorted was full of rat poison.

Officer Dayes clicked off the report and looked over at Devon Adams.

"Have there been any other cocaine poisoning deaths besides Hillman's?" she asked.

Adams shook his head. "No. Which is kind of strange. If it was a poisoned batch we should have seen other deaths, but Hillman is the only one. So far anyway."

Glory shook her head in disgust. "It's bad enough these drug dealers get their customers hooked on the stuff, but they use poison to cut it. Why would they want to limit their sales?"

"Usually they don't," said Adams picking up his coffee cup. After he took a sip, he grimaced. "Must be that they were worried about Belinda. She was pretty messed up after years of using. They probably figured she's give away information if she was picked up again."

"Of course. Hook them, burn them out, then get rid of them. What foul characters they must be," said Glory.

"Hey, they're drug dealers, what do you expect? They're not boy scouts."

The dispatcher from the front buzzed Glory's phone. "Officer Dayes could you come to the front desk, please?" asked Sheila.

Surprised, Glory said she'd be right there. She looked at Adams. "You haven't heard about anything related to search and rescue, have you?"

He shrugged and shook his head without looking away from his computer screen.

When she got to the front she spotted a middle-aged man with short brown hair and a younger man with his red hair pulled back into a ponytail.

Sheila looked up at Glory. "These two gentlemen have something that might interest you. This is James Ford and Winston Prescott. Officer Glory Dayes may be able to help you," she told the men.

Glory shook hands with them. "Follow me this way to an interview room." She led the way down a long corridor past several offices.

Winston admired the view he had of the back of Officer Dayes. Even her gray uniform couldn't hide all the curves underneath it, especially her hips that swayed slightly as she walked. She was pretty and had a trim athletic build. He didn't think he'd ever met anyone with violet eyes before, a dark shade of purple that was very unusual. She was almost as tall as he was, probably five foot ten. He wondered how old she was. She looked barely old enough to have graduated high school.

Glory opened the door to a plain room with a table and four chairs, light gray, empty walls and no windows. "Have a seat and tell me why you think you need to talk to someone on the police dive team."

James pulled a blue swim fin out of the plastic bag he'd been carrying. "I'll let Winston tell you the story."

Winston cleared his throat and looked at her. "My dad, Richard Prescott, went missing two years ago. The Coast Guard searched for days but all they found was debris from his boat on the east side of Damariscove Island. No boat or body. Yesterday while we were diving the area we found this fin that belonged to my dad. James thinks that hole was made by a bullet."

Glory's face betrayed no signs of emotion. She picked up the fin and examined the hole. She held it up to the light. "Could be. How do you know this was your dad's?"

Winston reached across and turned the fin over. "That was the name of his boat."

She looked at the faded white paint. "OK. What made you suspect the hole was caused by a bullet?"

"I'm a private detective, former cop," informed James. "I've seen plenty of bullet holes."

She nodded. "Did you find anything else?"

Winston frowned and shook his head.

"I just recently joined the dive team," she said. "I'm not familiar with what happened to your father. Can you give me a few days to talk to the team and read about his case?"

Winston nodded. "I was hoping someone would at least look into this. If my dad was murdered, I'd hoped they'd start the search for his body."

Glory frowned. "After all this time I'm not sure there would be any point in that. He could have washed out to sea, or…"

Winston knew she was thinking a body would be eaten by now. "I know it's a long shot after all this time, but it would help my mom have some closure."

Glory's eyes softened. "I understand. Give me your phone number and I'll get back to you after I have time to do a little research." She stood up and handed him her card and a piece of paper and pen from off the table.

"Thank you for at least not blowing this off," said Winston, writing down his cell phone number. He added the house phone number, too. "If you can't reach me, my mom's usually at this number at home."

Glory took them back to the front and watched them leave. The young guy was kind of cute, she thought. Must either work out or be a lobsterman. The broad shoulders and thick arm muscles were a dead give away.

Back at her desk she pulled up the old case on her computer. There was not much to read about Richard Prescott. The fruitless search had lasted a week. No sign of boat or body or foul play. It was ruled accidental drowning. But where was the boat? If it went down anywhere near the debris the divers should have found it.

After lunch she went to talk to the lead detective on the Prescott case.

"It was a strange one," said Officer Brent West. "No signs of the boat having gotten broken up or gone down, just that debris floating in the water. If there'd been a storm the boat might have broke anchor and drifted out to sea, but the weather was calm that whole week. If the guy fell off his boat, maybe the sharks got him. Why are you asking?"

She showed him the swim fin and told him about her interview. "Can we re-open the case?" she asked.

West looked at the swim fin. "It could be a bullet hole or damage from something else. There's no way we can talk the powers-that-be into spending more money looking for the guy after two years," he said. "Besides the Coast Guard divers searched the area for miles all around that island for a week. Sorry."

She frowned. "What should I tell the family?"

He shrugged. "It's always hard for the family in a case like this. I'm afraid they'll have to be disappointed." He patted her shoulder. "This is the hard part of our job."

## Chapter 16

Parker looked at William. "Hey, Will, look at this. The cops finally found Belinda," he said holding up the newspaper with her obituary.

William grabbed the paper and scanned it. "Did you see any sign of a police report?"

"Nah, just this obit. Doesn't even say how she died."

Will smiled. "Good. Don't want to scare off any customers." He went back to eating his three egg McMuffins from McDonalds.

"When we gonna get rid of that guy's boat?" asked Parker. He was still nervous having the *Chelsea* stored in the boat shed in back of the house. "Don't you think the heat's off it by now? It's been two frickin' years."

Will swallowed the last bite of his breakfast and finished his beer before answering. "Yeah, I guess you're right. I've got a buyer up on Prince Edward's Island waiting for it. Guess I should give him a call."

Late that afternoon Will dropped anchor off the coast of PEI outside Murray Harbor. Richard's boat had a new blue paint job and new name. *Sunset View* stood out in black letters on the back end of the boat.

Parker pulled up beside the lobster boat in Will's fancy new speedboat and dropped anchor to wait. After seeing Earl Childs' speedboat, Will decided he wanted one. It was a lot more fun than his fishing boat. His wasn't as expensive or as big as Earl's, but it could fly over the waves and suited him just fine.

Will waved at Parker and nodded.

Within thirty minutes a small dinghy pulled up beside Richard's stolen boat. A tall man with a dark beard and mustache grinned as he climbed on board. He waved at the driver of the dinghy and it drove off.

After Marcel Thibodeaux walked around the boat examining every detail Will asked, "Well, isn't it everything I told you?"

"It's even nicer than the photos," said Marcel as he pulled open cabinets and looked at the storage areas. "May I try it out?"

"Certainly." Will pulled up the anchor and Marcel started the engine.

Marcel sped off toward open water. After driving around for ten minutes and trying out the radio, he returned to the harbor. He handed Will an envelope full of American currency. "So nice doing business with you," he smiled. "I'm always looking for more boats."

Will stuffed the envelope in the waistband of his pants. "If I come across any more bargains, I'll let you know," he said waving for Parker to bring the speedboat closer. Parker dropped the bumper between the two vessels and Will jumped on to the deck of his boat.

Before Parker got the speedboat turned around, Marcel sped away toward the dock.

Will sat down and pulled out the envelope. A stack of hundred dollar bills was crammed inside. After counting the bills he grinned. "Not bad for an old lobster boat."

"How much did you get?" yelled Parker over the roar of the boat engine. Pushing the speed higher he headed south. He was nervous in foreign waters and wanted to get away from Canada as fast as possible.

"Eighteen thousand five hundred," said Will. "I'm just happy to be rid of it. The boat was the only thing connecting us to that diver."

"I wonder what ever happened to him," called Parker.

Will shrugged. "I know I shot him. He's long gone by now."

Parker nodded. Poor sap washed out to sea and probably got eaten by sharks, he thought. It wasn't like they had anything against the guy; just wrong place, wrong time.

It was close to sunset by the time they reached Will's private dock. They secured the boat and hurried inside. Will made arrangements to meet up with a couple of hookers at a local bar in an hour. He wanted to have a shower before that appointment.

Parker headed home with a promise to meet him and the women at ten o'clock.

Will walked into the bar at nine-forty. He wore a nice pair of black slacks and a gray pullover shirt. His brown hair was slicked back. Two little bags of coke were tucked in his pocket. The girls liked to use it. He never touched the stuff. He saw on a daily basis what it did to your body. Sure he drank beer, but he didn't touch the hard stuff. His body was a temple and he enjoyed how it worked for him. Booze and dope dulled the senses. He wanted his body on full alert and he enjoyed sex too much to dull the thrill.

Parker showed up at the same time as the women. He led them to Will's table in the back corner. Stacy wore a tight black dress with a slit up the side that stopped half way up her thigh. Her wavy bleached blond hair fell to her shoulders. She slid a chair up beside Will.

"Hi, Sugar," she giggled, planting a kiss on his cheek.

Will reached over and pulled her chair closer.

Cherry wore her curly brown hair cut in a cute bob. She had full red lips and blue eyes. She wore a red dress that barely covered her bottom. She had her arm through Parker's and only let go of him when he pulled out her chair.

Parker sat down and whispered in her ear causing her to playfully slap him on the shoulder. "You're so naughty," she quipped in a soft sexy voice.

Parker's blond hair was spiked up with gel and he wore a new pair of jeans, a button up Western shirt and a pair of cowboy boots. Sometimes Parker wished he lived in Texas.

Both girls ordered rum and coke and a couple of appetizers.

By eleven o'clock the girls were anxious to get to the hotel. They'd seen Will flash the bags and they wanted a snort. Will and Parker were only too glad to oblige.

Chapter 17

"Winston Prescott?" said a female voice when Winston answered his phone.

"Yes."

"This is Officer Dayes. I'm afraid I have bad news," said Glory. "The police don't feel that the swim fin is enough evidence of foul play to re-open your father's case."

"I kind of figured as much," said Winston.

She could tell he was disappointed and she felt bad. "They didn't find anything two years ago and they wouldn't know where else to search. I'm so sorry."

"If I find anything else I'll let you know. I plan to do another dive in the area."

She wanted to say something to make him feel better and she impulsively added, "If you love to dive as much as I do, you might enjoy diving at Fort Foster in Kittery. There's an old military fortress on shore."

"I've been to that site once with my dad years ago," he said. "It was pretty cool."

"Oh. Well if you're experienced enough there's a great spot off Eastport. It's the site of the old steamship pier. Campobello Island, Canada is right across the way and there's all kinds of neat stuff to see," she said. "I've found things that were thrown in the water off the pier years ago. Stuff like clay pipes and old medicine bottles."

"That does sound fun." He was silent for a minute.

"Are you still there?" she asked.

"I was wondering if you go diving for fun or just for work."

"I haven't been out for fun much lately," she admitted. "I just recently made it on the dive team. It was a lot of work and it kept me pretty busy. And the two friends I used to dive with are married and have a kid now. So they're pretty busy."

"Since you're not investigating my case, would it be against policy for you to dive with me?" he tried not to let his voice show how nervous he was asking her. She was beautiful, out of his league and a cop.

"I don't see any reason why I couldn't dive with you. I'd love to show you the pier. It's really one of my favorite spots to dive," she said. "The currents can be pretty strong there. It's best to go at high tide."

"That would be great," he said, amazed that she'd said yes.

"I'll have to get back to you when I find out my schedule."

"Sure, I understand. I spend most days out hauling lobster traps on my boat, but I keep my phone with me. When I'm near shore I can get reception," he said. "Or you could call in the evening."

"You have your own boat?"

"Yeah. It's nothing fancy. Just a lobster boat, but it's only two years old and it can get us to Eastport on the water," he said. "We wouldn't have to drive up there."

"That saves a lot of time," she said. "The water's pretty darn cold up there. Do you have a dry-suit?"

"I do. My dad insisted we use them. He was always worried about hypothermia," he said. "My cousin's up visiting for the summer and he can go with us. Safety in numbers, you know."

"Ok, then. I'll get back with you when I know my schedule." As she disconnected the call she inwardly cringed. Crap, did she just agree to go diving with civilians? She sat at her desk thinking about Winston. He seemed like an intelligent, nice guy. And he was certainly good to look at. She'd dive with him this time and see what happened. Unfortunately she'd been fooled before and she didn't want to get into another bad relationship.

Winston sat in a daze for several seconds after the call finished. Officer Dayes agreed to go diving with him. Even in his wildest dreams he hadn't imagined that. He'd been thinking about her all morning. Well, don't get your hopes up he chided himself. She's just being nice to some poor schmuck because she felt bad that the cops wouldn't open his dad's case.

Michel looked in Winston's open bedroom door. His hair was still wet from his shower and he was toweling it dry. "You're looking happy this morning. What happened?"

Winston grinned. "Officer Dayes called."

"Are they going to open the case again?"

Winston shook his head.

"Oh, then why are you grinning?"

"She said she'd go diving with us," said Winston.

"Who did?" asked Michel pulling on a pair of jeans.

"Officer Glory Dayes."

"Glory Days? What kind of name is that?" asked Michel.

Winston threw the pillow from his bed at Michel. "I don't care what her name is. You weren't with us so you didn't see her," said Winston catching the pillow when Michel lobbed it back at him. "She's intelligent and gorgeous and she love to dive. What more could I want?"

Michel grinned. "Oh, so that's why you have that silly grin on your face." He ducked when the pillow came flying at him again.

"Hey, I can't wait to see your face when you meet her."

"So I get to go diving with the two of you?" he asked.

"Yeah, it's always safer to have at least three divers. She told me about this great place up near Eastport. Besides this isn't a date or anything. I figure it's a pity dive," admitted Winston. "But I don't care. It will be worth it."

####

A week later Glory's schedule opened giving her three days off. Of course she would be on call if a rescue mission came up, but she was tired off sitting in the office with nothing going on. When she didn't have a dive mission, she had to do routine police work which basically meant a lot of paperwork for mundane stuff.

She agreed to meet Winston at the Rockport Harbor and they would take his boat to the dive site near Eastport. It was barely seven when she parked her Camry and walked down to the pier carrying her dry-suit, fins and a picnic basket. Winston spotted her and waved, then hurried over to help.

Glory wore a blue one-piece bathing suit that hugged her curves and an unbuttoned long-sleeve shirt over the suit. Her black hair was pulled back in a braid.

Winston took the basket and smiled. "Looks like it's going to be nice weather," he said. He wore black swim trunks and a t-shirt that strained against his chest and muscular arms.

"I still need to get my air tank out of the car," she said.

"I have a couple of extra tanks and I filled all of them this morning," he said. We probably don't need yours unless you want it."

"Oh, it's nothing special. I can use yours."

When they reached the boat Winston handed the picnic basket to Michel who set it down then extended his hand to help Glory step from the dock to the boat deck.

"Glory Dayes, this is Michel Woods, my second cousin from Arkansas."

"Nice to meet you." She looked around the boat then walked to the cabin. The boat had all the modern electronic equipment he needed including a state-of-art radio. "This is a nice setup you've got here, Winston."

"Thanks, Mom insisted on that radio after dad went missing. She's still a little nervous about me taking over dad's traps."

Glory nodded.

Winston loosened the ropes attached to the dock and jumped on board. "We cleaned the boat up yesterday. It can sometimes get a little ripe with all the fish and lobsters on board."

She smiled. "You didn't have to go to all that trouble. I've been on lobster boats before."

He shrugged. "No, trouble." He stepped into the cabin and started the engine while Michel pushed away from the dock with a long pole. "I figure it will take us about three hours to get to the site. That puts us right at slack high tide."

"Good. The currents are strong in Passamaquoddy Bay. Divers only go down at slack high or low tide. I've heard of divers getting caught in a riptide if they stay down too long. So that gives us only about forty-five minutes to explore," she said. "You both are experienced divers, right?"

They both nodded. "I've dived with my dad a lot," said Michel.

"That's good," she said taking a seat in one of the chairs.

Winston began maneuvering the boat away from the harbor. Most of the other fishing and lobster boats were out working.

Glory took a deep breath enjoying the salty air and sunshine. "We'll be fine as long as we stay close to the bottom when we dive. If you feel yourself being pulled by the water currents you can grab hold of a big rock and push out of the stream," she explained. "This is one of my favorite dives but I haven't been there in several years."

While Winston drove the boat, Glory unpacked the picnic basket and handed out fried egg sandwiches and bottles of juice. They enjoyed the warmth as the sun rose higher. The blue sky held a few fluffy white clouds and seagulls passed by in flocks making a racket with their squawking. After they ate, she packed up the trash papers, put on her sunglasses and went to sit at the back of the boat. She loved being out on the water.

It was hard to hear over the engine noise and Michel stood close to Winston in the cabin to talk. "You didn't tell me she was knock-out gorgeous," he said grinning. "Wow! And she's a cop? Holy cow, I wouldn't mind being arrested by her."

Winston's grin spread from ear to ear. "I know." He glanced back at Glory and she waved. "I still can't believe she's on my boat."

The hours it took to reach the dive site flew by as they enjoyed the boat ride and watched the sea life around them. They watched the cormorants, large black birds, diving for fish with their long curved beaks.

Michel was the first one to spot a humpback whale. He pointed it out to Glory.

"Gosh, that's a big one," she said shielding her eyes from the sun as they watched the whale splash out of the water.

They reached the shore of Eastport by ten-thirty. The ocean was calm and deep at slack high tide. They hurriedly dropped anchor, donned their dry-suits and helped each other with the tanks. Dropping carefully over the side, they sank into the cold water. Kicking with her fins, Glory led them straight to the rocky bottom.

For the next forty minutes they swam with lumpfish and the occasional seal. Winston was surprised by all the sea life so far north. Although the water had a greenish cast from all the plankton, the visibility was still a good fifteen feet. The undersea life was explosive with color; bright orange starfish, pale beige Basket starfish, pink sea anemones and yellow coral amidst the waving dark green kelp beds. Small schools of fish swam by brushing against the divers.

Hermit crabs and striped shrimp swam over scallops and clams resting on the ocean floor.

Michel swam close and touched Winston's arm then pointed to a huge lobster outside a rock cave eating something. It looked to weigh at least six pounds.

Glory waved them over to see a giant Atlantic wolf fish. It peered at them from between two big rocks, its dark gray stripes alternating with lighter gray stripes. It was obviously accustomed to divers and was so friendly it let her pet the top of its head.

Their time was running short and Winston pointed to his underwater watch. They each nodded and began to kick toward the surface. When they surfaced they were fifty feet from the boat. They ducked back underwater and swam toward the overhead shadow of the boat.

Michel was the first to break water and he grabbed the short ladder on the back of the boat to haul himself up. After removing his mask and mouthpiece, he reached down and helped Glory climb on board. Winston heaved himself up and the three of them helped each other remove the air tanks and get out of their dive gear.

"That was fantastic!" said Winston, handing out bottles of water from the cooler. "I can't believe all of that is on the coast of Maine. I've dived a lot of sites but I've never seen so much color. I thought places like this were only in warm water."

Glory grinned. "I know. Isn't it great? That's why I love this place."

"What's with that big fish you petted?" asked Michel

"That's '*Gene the wolf fish*'. He's not afraid of divers and will even eat out of your hand if you have a snack for him," she said. "He's a local attraction."

While Glory squeezed the water out of her braid with a towel, Winston pulled out his lunch cooler.

"It's time for lunch," said Winston. "Mom packed ton's of food."

They rested on deck eating the fried chicken, potato salad, homemade cookies and fresh rolls Annette packed for their lunch. Glory sat back in her deck chair and shook her head when Winston offered her another piece of chicken.

"If I eat another bite I'll explode," she laughed. "Your mom's a great cook. Be sure and tell her for me. I don't do a lot of cooking myself and I appreciate someone who does."

After they finished eating, Winston headed the boat back home. They pulled up to the Rockport dock at three o'clock. Winston and Michel helped Glory carry her things to her car.

"That was fun," she said smiling. "I had a wonderful time. We'll have to do this again sometime."

"Thanks for showing us your favorite dive spot," said Winston.

"No problem. Next time we'll have to dive a sunken ship," she said. "There are dozens of them out there if you know where to look."

"Really? That sounds great."

The two men reluctantly watched her drive away then headed back to the boat to load the equipment in the back of Winston's truck.

"Man, I'd go diving anywhere with her," said Michel wistfully.

"Too bad you're heading home this fall," laughed Winston.

That earned him a punch in the arm.

## Chapter 18

Everyone was sitting around Annette's table eating breakfast early one morning. Today there were mounds of scrambled eggs, ham slices and raisin toast.

"I can't believe we've been here five weeks already," said Lacey. "Aren't you getting tired of us yet, Annette?"

Annette shook her head and swallowed a bite. "Nope, you can stay until you have to go back when Lily's school starts. Besides, I still haven't taken you to all the great places to see in Maine. We haven't even made it down to Reed State Park or Popham Beach or Old Orchard Beach. I'm not tired of having company yet."

Lacey shook her head and smiled. "As long as you keep letting me pay for the groceries, we're happy to stay. Otherwise we'd eat you out of house and home before long."

"You have to stay until the first weekend in August," said Winston. "That's when we have the Lobster Fest. People from all over New England come each year."

"What's the Lobster Fest?" asked Lily, pausing before taking a bite of toast. Today she wore a *Little Mermaid* t-shirt that was getting too small. She wasn't ready to give it up yet.

"It's a festival down in Rockland on the harbor with craft booths, lobster dinners, a carnival and all sorts of fun. It's a volunteer event to raise money for local charities. Last year they raised $500,000," explained Winston. "This year I'm competing in the trap race."

Lily looked confused. "What's a trap race?"

Winston laughed. "Wooden lobster traps are attached together and strung out on ropes stretched across the water in the harbor. Contestants have to run across the floating traps without falling off. It's fun to watch and I almost made it to the end last year."

Lily's eyes were wide open in surprise. "Wow, that sounds hard."

"It is hard," laughed Annette. "The traps float and move around so much it's hard to stay on top of them. Most people don't make it halfway across before falling in the water. Winston is also one of the suppliers of the lobsters they cook at the festival every year. *Atwood*'s has a big lobster pound where the lobsters are kept alive for weeks until the festival. Last year they sold 19,000 pounds of lobster. They also serve other seafood, clam and lobster chowders and Maine blueberry pancakes."

Lily looked at her mother and grinned.

Lacey laughed. "Yes, you can have some pancakes."

Later Lacey was helping Annette clean up the dishes after breakfast.

Annette asked, "I hate to ask while you're all here on vacation, but do you think James would help a friend of mine?"

"I'm sure he'd be glad to help. He's getting a little bored with tourist stuff about now. What's the problem?" asked Lacey, drying her hands after putting the last dish in the dishwasher. "No, wait a minute, let me get James, he'll want to hear this."

The two of them met Annette on the back porch a few minutes later.

"Tell James what you were going to tell me," said Lacey sitting beside James on the porch swing.

"OK. My friend Sally Winsome is a single mom with three little kids. Her mother passed away a few years ago and since then she's been helping her father run his hardware store," explained Annette. "He passed away from cancer in May. It was really hard on her to lose him and to make matters worse no one can find his will. Her brother wants her to sell the store and split the money with him. But her father had told her she would inherit the store since she was the only one who helped him after her mother died."

"I'm assuming she's checked with his lawyer," said James.

"He didn't use a lawyer. He wrote up his will using one of those Lawyer app thingy's."

James frowned. "Did he get it notarized and witnessed?"

"She said he did. But she can't find his copy." Annette pressed her lips together. "Do you think you could help her?"

"Well, Lacey and I have found a lot of missing items over the years. We could at least give it a try."

Annette smiled. "That's wonderful. We can go to the store and you could meet her right now. The store opened at eight o'clock."

They drove downtown to Rockland and parked on the street in front of *Winsome's Hardware Store* located in an old red brick building with a big front window displaying merchandise. There were sets of tools, fishing supplies, pots of flowers, cans of paint and brushes neatly displayed in the window.

A little bell chimed when they opened the front door. There were no customers inside at the moment. Rows of tools, boxes of nails, screws, bolts and hinges of all sizes filled the front aisles. Shovels for digging dirt and shoveling snow leaned against one wall. On another wall fishing supplies filled the whole area; life jackets, waders, rods and reels of varying sizes, spinners, lures and supplies for making your own flies to catch trout. At the back of the store were various gardening supplies; clay pots, tools, gloves, fertilizers and racks of seed packets.

Sally came out of the back office and met them up front. Her honey blond hair was cut short and she wore stylish glasses that framed her hazel eyes. She had on little makeup and wore an apron with the store logo over her jeans and shirt.

Annette made introductions then stood back to let James question Sally.

"Did your father have a safety deposit box at his bank?" he asked.

"Not that I know of and I've looked," Sally admitted. "There is a wall safe somewhere in the store but I haven't been able to find it yet." She sighed. "He said I would have the store and my brother would get his house. But Trent wants to sell both and use the money."

"What grounds does Trent have for fighting you on this?" asked James.

"There's an older will dad made back when we were teenagers. It split everything fifty-fifty. Neither one of us were interested in the store back then. We had big plans to go to college and leave Maine. Trent dropped out of college and now works with a deep-sea fishing crew. I ended up pregnant my senior year in high school and got married." She sighed. "Three kids later, Steve and I got divorced. He moved to Virginia and remarried. We don't hear much from him."

"So your father made a new will when you started working here?"

Sally nodded. "After my mother died and I began working with dad. We were both lonely and it was a good solution. I've grown to love ordering supplies and trying out new things in the store. I don't want to sell it and have to find a job somewhere else."

Annette nodded in sympathy.

"The store is all I have left of my folks," said Sally wiping at a tear on her cheek. "My kids are all little right now. Angel is seven, Joe's four and Annie's only two. I have a cousin who babysits for me and is willing to care for them at my house. It's a great situation for right now. When the kids get older, they could work with me here." She sighed. "If I have to find another job it probably won't pay as much either. The store does a lot of business."

Just then the bell over the door dinged and she went to help a customer. While Sally showed the man fishing supplies, the three of them moved to the back of the store to talk.

"I suppose I could spend some time here looking for the wall safe," said James. "There has to be a computer he used to keep track of the business, Lacey could look through that. It might have some information that would point to a bank deposit box Sally doesn't know about."

They waited while Annette rang up the man's sale. He purchased over three hundred dollars worth of fishing supplies.

"Have you decided you can help me?" asked Sally. "I insist on paying your going rate."

James smiled. "We can figure that out if we find the will. I'll hang around today and look for the safe. Lacey is my computer guru and she wants to take a look at the office computer."

Sally's face split into a huge grin. "That's great. Thanks for finding help for me Annette."

"Call me when you're finished here," said Annette. "I have a few errands to run and I'll take Lily with me so the guys can head out on the boat."

"Tell Winston thanks for waiting on us this morning so Michel could keep an eye on Lily. I know he usually likes to get out early," said Lacey.

Sally took Lacey back to the office and gave her the password to get into the computer. After James scoured the walls of the store but found nothing, he headed to the back storeroom to look for the wall safe.

The store had a rush of customers and Sally was busy all morning. At eleven-thirty she had a break and went to check on Lacey.

"I found the original document your father made for the new will," Lacey told her. "But he had to print it off and get it notarized and witnessed to make it legal." Lacey showed her where she'd found the will. "It was in this folder with some other letters."

Sally frowned. "I guess it won't help me much, will it?"

"It shows his intent, but it's not legal."

"Dang it." She sighed. "I have to find the printed one."

About that time they heard James hollering from the storeroom. They hurried to the back room to see what he found.

James was grinning as he waved them over to the back wall. "I finally noticed that this old advertising poster wasn't tacked down on the end," he said, lifting the edge of the poster. "Here's the safe. Do you have any idea what the combination is?"

Sally's eyebrows drew together as she concentrated. "Try my mother's birthday. August 4th, 1954."

James slowly spun the dial but nothing happened.

"Try dad's birthday." She told him the date but it didn't work either.

"Try their anniversary."

This time a small click could be heard as James entered the last number. He stepped back and let Sally open the door. Inside was a small stack of bound one hundred dollar bills. "Dad's emergency money," she said, putting it on a nearby shelf.

There was the title to her father's work truck, the deed to the store, which was completely paid off, and a life insurance policy. She held up the policy.

The policy was a term life insurance for $100,000. "I didn't even know he had this." But there was no will. Sally sighed. "Darn, I was sure it would be in the safe."

"Is there any place at his house where he might have stashed it?" asked James.

"I don't know. I'll give you the keys and maybe you could check it out this afternoon," said Sally handing him a key. "Do you have time to look today?"

"Sure." He pocketed the key.

Sally looked at Lacey. "Dad has a laptop computer at the house. You could see if there's anything on that. Maybe by some wild chance he scanned in the signed will," she said. "He always used the same password that he used here."

"We'll head over there after lunch," promised Lacey. "First I'd like to go home and check on Lily."

## Chapter 19

William Furman was sitting on his front porch enjoying a beer when the sound of a car engine attracted his attention. He spotted a bright red TransAm at the end of his street headed his way. He was astonished when it roared into his driveway.

"What the hell?" he muttered standing up from his chair. He started to yell at the driver to get off his property when the front door of the vehicle opened.

Parker Thomas stepped out of the car. He had a huge grin on his face as he waved to Will. "What do you think?" he hollered. "Isn't she a beauty?"

Parker had on new jeans and a shiny new pair of alligator leather cowboy boots.

Will stomped down the porch steps. "You idiot! Don't tell me you bought that car!"

Parker took a step back. Then he got angry and jutted out his chin. "So what if I did!"

Will grabbed Parker by the arm and hustled him into the house. His face was beet red as Will slammed the front door behind them.

"I told you not to do anything stupid," Will hissed. "Driving around in a town as small as Rockland in that thing is bound to attract attention."

"So what! The chicks really dig it," said Parker. He stepped back and shoved Will's hand off his arm. "It was my money."

Will clenched his hands to keep from punching Parker in the face. "We talked about this, Parker," he said as calmly as he could. "We weren't going to throw money around. It attracts the attention of the police. Remember? We talked about this last week."

Parker pouted. "Yeah I remember. But you bought that fancy speedboat. Why can't I buy a nice car?"

Will gave an exasperated sigh. "That's not a nice car; that is a police magnet! Don't be so stupid, Parker."

"But your boat's just as flashy!" protested Parker. "And don't call me stupid! You know I graduated high school."

Will nodded. "You're right. I'm sorry. You're not stupid. Just too impulsive sometimes," he said trying to smooth Parker's ruffled feathers. "My boat is out on the water where nobody sees it. That bright red car attracts attention, Parker."

Parker sighed. "Yeah, lots of people waved when I drove downtown."

Will rolled his eyes. "How did you pay for it?"

Parker looked at the floor. "With cash."

Will shook his head. "And you don't think that would make the car dealer a little suspicious, paying cash?"

"Well, I told him I had a rich uncle who died and left me a lot of money," said Parker looking up and feeling smart.

Will walked over to the recliner and sat down. "Do you think the cops will buy that lie the first time they pull you over?"

Parker shrugged. "Maybe."

"They'll want to know your uncle's name. They can check out your story, Parker." Will took a deep breath. "I'm sorry, but you can't drive around in that bright red car and not attract attention from the cops. You have to take it back."

"Ah, Will. I don't want to take it back," whined Parker. "I already named her Reba. Cause you know Reba McEntire has red hair."

"I know you love Reba's country music," said Will. "But a red car is too flashy. You don't want to blow our cover, do you?"

Parker shook his head. "No. But what good is having bundles of money if we can't spend it? Huh, Will? You got a smart answer for that?"

Will rubbed his hand down his face. Parker did have a point. "Look, we've got gobs of dough. How about we take a vacation? We could spend money in Miami or Las Vegas and nobody would be the wiser."

"Really, we could go on vacation? We never went on vacation before," said Parker.

"So you'll take the red car back?"

Parker nodded. "No red car, got it."

Will patted him on the back. "Did the dealer tell you there was a grace period?"

"Huh? What's that?"

"A certain length of time when you could change your mind about the car."

Parker nodded. "Yeah, he said if I didn't like driving it I could return in before ten days was up. I just got it yesterday, so I can still take it back."

"That's good. So go do that right now."

"Alright." Parker left. He wasn't happy about taking his dream car back, but if Will was going to take him on vacation, maybe it was worth it.

Will thought he'd handled that well. At least Parker hadn't been driving around in that thing for days. He made himself a sandwich and went back out on the porch to eat lunch. He'd finished the last bite when a car pulled into his driveway.

Parker had exchanged the TransAm for a dark blue Camaro. He had a big grin on his face as he walked to the porch. "What do you think?"

Will sighed. "Parker, it's still pretty flashy."

Parker frowned. "It isn't red," he protested.

Will sighed. "Yeah, it's a nice color. But you should buy a little economy car that blends in with all the other cars around here. Or a truck, like mine."

"But I don't want a truck."

"Ok, never mind. But try not to speed or attract the cops."

Parker's face split into a huge grin. "Then I can keep it?"

Will patted his shoulder. "Yeah, you can keep it. But it might be a good idea to park it in your garage at night. You wouldn't want anyone to steal it."

That made them both laugh. After a few minutes they sobered up. It was the junkies they hooked that created most of the crime in the area.

"You got a point," admitted Parker. "When are we going to Vegas?"

## Chapter 20

James used the key Sally gave him to open the front door to her father's house. The air was musty and hot inside, evidence that it hadn't been open in a while. Lacey walked in behind him. "We better open some windows," she said. "I can't work in this heat."

They went around opening windows and the cool sea air helped dispel some of the heat. The house was a three-bedroom, two-story saltbox only a block from the ocean. The furniture was old, but everything was clean and orderly.

"I'll start looking around for a safe," said James. "Sally said his laptop was in the front bedroom."

She nodded and headed down the hallway. The front bedroom had been converted into an office. There was an old oak desk, a comfortable office chair and a set of metal file cabinets. An old tan loveseat sat against one wall with embroidered pillows and a crocheted blanket on it.

Lacey booted up the laptop and began her search for the elusive will. There were dozens of icons on the desktop. Lacey shook her head. Sally's father had downloaded tons of apps and programs. It would take a while to go through them all.

James didn't have much luck finding a wall safe. He checked behind paintings and framed family photos on the walls in all the front rooms. The office where Lacey worked had none and neither did the other bedrooms.

James rubbed his forehead. Where else could he look? Then a thought hit him. Maybe there was a floor safe. He's seen them before in other old houses, especially if there was a basement as that left room under the floorboards. So he went back to the living room and started checking under the throw rugs and room-size carpets. After thirty minutes of fruitless searching he ended up in the master bedroom again.

He checked under the two area rugs. Nothing. He opened the door to the closet and noticed a rug under the row of shoes and boots. Hastily moving the footwear out of his way, he lifted the corner of the rug. And there sat a floor safe with a recessed dial.

James pulled a piece of paper out of his pocket and began trying different numbered dates to see if one of them would open the safe.

Lacey had made her way through twenty folders when one stuck in the corner of the screen caught her eye. It was labeled "my treasures". She clicked on the folder and it opened to reveal other folders. The first one was full of digital family photos. Some of them were black and white and quite old. So at least Sally's father did know how to use a scanner. Another folder held scans of insurance papers and deeds. The will was in the third folder she opened.

Lacey held her breath as she clicked through the pages to see if it was an original unsigned document or if it was a scanned legal one. The last scanned page showed a notary seal and two witness' signatures. She spontaneously gave out a holler.

At the same time Lacey found the scanned document, James found the correct combination for the safe. He lifted the metal door and pulled out two documents; the deed for the house and the will. He hurriedly turned to the back page where he spotted the notary seal and witness' signatures.

He rushed to the hall and nearly bumped into Lacey. "I found it!" they said simultaneously. James handed her the will and Lacey laughed.

"I just found the scanned version," she said hugging James. "Sally will be thrilled.

####

Winston came home early from pulling his lobster traps. He showered and shaved and was wearing clean jeans, a button up shirt and polished shoes when he came downstairs. His mother whistled at him when he walked into the kitchen.

"Don't you look nice," she said. "Going some place special?"

"I thought I'd stop by the police station for a few minutes," he said nonchalantly.

"Oh, really?" she said grinning. "Going to see Glory?"

He nodded self-consciously. "She's been out diving with me and Michel three times now, but that's not a date. So I don't know how she feels about me."

"And how do you feel about her?" asked Annette, straightening his collar and brushing imaginary lint off his shoulder.

He blushed. "Mom, I think she's fantastic. But she's too good for me. She's educated, beautiful and a career woman. Why would she want to date a lowly lobsterman?"

Annette hugged him. "You are a handsome, intelligent man. It doesn't matter that you're not some fancy big shot. I loved your dad with all my heart and he was a lobsterman."

"Yeah, but you're a special woman," he protested.

"Well, maybe Glory is a special woman, too. So you're going to ask her out on a real date?" she asked.

"I want to ask her to go to the Lobster Fest with us. Does that count as a date?" he asked.

"Hmm, with the whole family and kin? Won't that be too much for a first date?"

He winced. "Do you think so?"

"Why don't you first ask her out to dinner, to see if she's even interested?" suggested Annette. "You can spring the rest of us on her later if that works out."

He nodded. "Good idea."

The police station was busy when Winston arrived. The phones were ringing and two people waited up front. He tried not to listen, but being in the same room he couldn't help but overhear their conversation.

A tall skinny man with gray hair wearing worn overalls sat on the wooden bench against the wall. He had an under-bite that made his chin protrude forward like a bulldog's. He hugged a woman with short gray hair. "Don't worry," he said. "They'll find him."

"But he's been gone all night," she whispered sadly.

Winston wondered if there was a 'search and rescue' operation going on. If that were the case, Glory wouldn't be here. Just as he thought that, Glory walked out from the back offices.

She was beautiful even with no makeup and wearing her gray uniform. She looked surprised when she saw Winston and nodded to him as she walked over to the older couple.

"Mr. and Mrs. Thompson, they found Buster," she said smiling. "An officer is bringing him to the station for you. They should be here any minute."

The woman grabbed Glory by the hand. "Thank you so much. We surely wouldn't know what to do without him," she said with a catch in her voice.

At that moment the front door opened. A uniformed officer led an old collie in on a leash. The collie's eyes were clouded white. The dog lifted his nose in the air and sniffed. He barked and pulled against the leash trying to reach the couple as they hurried forward toward him.

The man leaned over and rubbed the dog behind the ears. "There you are fellow," he said cheerfully. He looked at the officer and smiled. "Thank you kindly. This poor old dog can barely see. We've had him for almost eighteen years, and occasionally he still gets into trouble just like when he was a pup."

The dog pushed up against the man's leg and whined.

The woman got down on her knees and hugged the dog's neck. "Poor thing, you must be starving. Let's get you home."

The officer handed the man the leash and the couple hurried out of the station.

Glory walked over to Winston. She smiled when he raised his eyebrows.

"Buster likes to chase squirrels," she laughed. "This time he went too far and got lost in the woods. He's almost blind and he couldn't find his way home last night."

"I saw the white in his eyes," said Winston.

"He's got cataracts, poor thing. But the vet says he's too old to go through surgery," she explained. "We have to go out and find him once in a while. The Thompson's are both too old to go chasing after him."

Glory looked Winston up and down. "What are you all dressed up for?" she asked.

Winston grinned. "Well, you see I had this idea of asking someone out for dinner and I thought I should at least look my best," he said.

"This is your best?" she asked, walking around him. "Not bad. You clean up pretty good."

"So I look good enough to ask her?"

She nodded. "Who is this lucky woman?"

"Well, her name is Glory Dayes," he said. "Do you think she'll say yes?"

Glory scrunched up her face. "Depends on where you plan to take her to eat."

"How about any place she wants to go?"

She nodded. "That would work. When is this dinner date?"

"Well, she'll have to check her schedule," he said. "I'm available any night."

Glory pulled a small calendar out of a pocket in her uniform. "Looks like next Thursday night's open. Would it be with just you, no Michel?"

For a second Winston faltered. "Ah, yeah, just me."

"Good. They say three's a crowd on a date," she quipped.

Winston unsuccessfully tried to restrain his grin. "How about seven o'clock? Where do you want to go?"

She smiled. "There's a nice seafood place in Camden. Would you want to pick me up or have me meet you there?"

"I'll pick you up," he said.

"OK, see you at seven on Thursday," she said, turning to leave. "Don't be late, I'm big on punctuality."

He saluted. "Yes, Ma'am. Oh, I mean Officer Dayes."

Winston practically floated out the station door.

The desk sergeant waved Glory over closer as she walked by the desk.

"He finally asked you out?" asked Sergeant Selma Benson.

Glory nodded. "I was beginning to think we would only be dive buddies," she said. "Or else I was going to have to ask him out."

"You're right," said Selma. "He is darn cute."

"Told you." Glory walked back down the hall smiling.

## Chapter 21

Winston's dinner date with Glory had gone even better than he hoped. The food was delicious and the restaurant service exceptional. The usual nervousness of a first date hadn't happened because they were already good friends from their dives together.

Winston wore a pale gray dress-shirt and black slacks. His green eyes sparkled when she opened the door to her apartment that night. She wore a rose colored dress of soft knit that clung to her body in all the right places. The cut was modest with a hem that fell to her knees but it still looked ravishing on her. Her shiny black hair fell in curls to her shoulders. Her thick black lashes required no mascara but she'd used a little blush to highlight her cheekbones.

They talked about everything. Winston learned Glory had a sister named Rose who was married and lived in New Hampshire. They laughed together as she told him about some of the antics of Rose's son, Josiah.

On the way home after dinner Winston asked if she would like to go to the Lobster Fest with him.

"It would be with my mother and all my visiting cousins," he said. "The Fords have never been to the festival so it will be fun watching their reactions. I'm competing in the trap race."

Her eyes widened. "You are? That should be fun to watch," she teased. "How far do you think you'll get?"

"Hey, I almost made it to the end last year," he protested. "I got to the last trap before my foot slipped."

She looked impressed. "That takes a lot of balance and dexterity. It's usually kids or little skinny guys that make it that far. I'd love to go and watch your attempt."

"Great. Which day works best for you? We're pretty open."

"I have Friday off that week."

"Friday it is then. I'll pick you up at ten o'clock," he said smiling.

It was close to nine-thirty that night when they arrived at Glory's apartment after dinner. There was the usual awkwardness at her front door until she gave him a quick kiss on the lips.

"I had a nice time. I have an early shift in the morning, so I'll have to call it a night," she said unlocking her door.

Winston's heart was pumping so frantically from the kiss he nodded and just said 'good night'. He barely slept that night thinking about her.

####

Friday the week of the Lobster Fest dawned bright and clear. The weather forecast was for a balmy eighty degrees with clear skies and sunshine. Down by the water it would feel cooler, but still be comfortable.

Lily woke at six o'clock and hurriedly dressed in shorts and a pink t-shirt. She buckled her sandals and crept into the hallway. With her father here now, Lily slept in a sleeping bag on the enclosed back porch. When she peeked in at her parents they were asleep but she heard little noises coming from the kitchen and hurried down the hall.

Annette was dressed and emptying the clean dishes from the dishwasher.

"Morning, Miss Annette," said Lily from the kitchen doorway.

"Well, I see you're up early," said Annette, putting the last bowl in the cupboard. "How does French toast for breakfast sound to you?"

"That sounds good, what time are we leaving for the Lobster Fest?" she asked pulling out a chair at the table and sitting down.

"We'll probably head over there around ten o'clock."

Lily huffed. "That's a long time from now."

Annette smiled. "I'll find something for you to do after breakfast so it won't seem so long. Do you want to help me make breakfast?"

Between the two of them they had breakfast on the table by seven-thirty when everyone else was awake and dressed. Lily was so excited she could barely eat, but that didn't stop Michel from putting away five pieces of French toast with bacon on the side.

Winston left shortly before ten to go pick up Glory.

Everyone else piled into the SUV and drove down to the Rockland Harbor. Music was already floating through the air when they arrived and parked the car. Long lines of people were crowding toward the entrance. Lily could barely contain her excitement when she saw the brightly colored canopies and carnival rides.

"How many rides can I go on?" she asked her mother.

"We'll have to see what's available and how much they cost," hedged Lacey.

Lily pouted. "Oh,"

James leaned over and whispered in Lily's ear. "I'll make sure you have fun."

Lily stepped closer to James and put her hand in his. He grinned. He was the prized parent today. It probably wouldn't last.

When they reached the front of the line, James insisted on paying for the tickets.

The smells of caramel popcorn, French fries and cooking seafood floated on the salty ocean breeze. Booths selling jewelry, crafts, different foods and clothing butted up against each other in long lines. Hundreds of people wandered from booth to booth enjoying the sights. Lacey quickly found a pair of silver starfish earrings she wanted. At the next booth she purchased a new *Little Mermaid* t-shirt in a bigger size for Lily.

Michel headed away from them to a booth that was selling knives and other manly souvenirs. Annette showed Lacey to her favorite booth selling homemade breads and muffins. Before they all became separated, James told everyone to meet back at the food tent at noon.

James watched over Lily in the bouncy house while the women looked through the different craft booths inside a large white tent. When she tired of jumping, Lily tried out a new ride that blew air up so hard from the rubber mat flooring that she floated up into the air tethered by a safety lease. Squealing with delight she waved her arms as her chestnut curls blew around her head.

Winston and Glory joined them at noon when it was time for lunch.

"Hey everyone, this is Glory Dayes," he said as they approached the reunited group standing in line at the lunch tent. "This is James and Lacey and their daughter, Lily. And this lovely woman is my mother, Annette."

Glory held out her hand, but instead of shaking it Annette pulled her into a hug.

Winston looked embarrassed. "I forgot to mention that my mother is a hugger."

Glory laughed. "No problem, my mother's a hugger, too." Glory bent down to talk to Lily. "I've heard a lot about you from Michel," she said smiling.

Lily's eyes widened and she glanced at Michel. "He probably told you all my secrets."

Glory laughed. "No, he told me how smart you are and what a nice little sister you were to him," she said. "What do you think about our festival?"

"I like it. I've never been to one like this."

The line started moving forward and soon it was their turn to enter the big food tent. The men all ordered the two-lobster dinner with corn on the cob and a roll. Lily wanted fried shrimp and Lacey got a lobster roll with fries. Annette and Glory ordered the lobster stew.

They found an empty picnic table and sat down. The women finished eating first and left the men to finish up their second lobsters while they wandered around to see more booths.

Toward the back of a cordoned off lot closer to the ocean they found something that positively thrilled Lily. An enormous clear glass bowl filled with water held a mermaid sitting on the edge of the bowl.

"Oh my gosh!" said Glory rushing forward. "I know that woman."

The mermaid's long dark red hair fell down her back in waves and her silvery fish tail sparkled in the sunshine. She wore a top with seashells on it and artificial flowers and seaweed were threaded through her hair. When she saw Glory, she smiled and waved.

When the others approached, Glory introduced them to the mermaid.

"This is my friend Mermaid Mera Jade, also known as Karin," said Glory.

Lily was thrilled and almost speechless as she walked up to the giant bowl. "I love mermaids," she said shyly.

"I know Karin from when she lived in Thomaston. She moved to Ohio and became a professional mermaid," said Glory. "Isn't she beautiful?"

Lily nodded her head in awe.

Mera Jade smiled down from her perch at Lily. "I've wanted to be a mermaid since I was a little girl," she said. "My mother sewed me my first tail when I was only four years old. I learned to swim underwater with it on."

"Wow," breathed out Lily. "That's awesome."

Mera Jade took off one of the bracelets that dangled on her arm and handed it to Lily. "This is a special mermaid bracelet," she said. "Since you're a special friend of Glory's, I want you to have it."

Lily accepted the silver bracelet with its tiny seahorses and starfish charms. "Can I really keep this?" she asked looking up at her mother.

"If Mera Jade wants you to have it, then you can keep it." Lacey smiled at the mermaid.

Lily slipped it on her wrist. "Thank you, Miss Mera Jade. Thank you so much."

A crowd began surrounding the bowl and the mermaid slipped down into the water. They watched as she swam in circles. When she pulled herself back onto the edge and offered to let people take photos with her, Lily rushed to the head of the line.

Lacey snapped several pictures then made Lily give up her spot to other awestruck little girls. Lily practically danced all the way back to the food tent. "I want to be a mermaid when I grow up," she declared.

The men were clearing away the trash from their meals when the group approached.

"Dad, look what I got," she said running up to James. "A real mermaid gave me this." She displayed the sparkling bracelet.

"Wow, that's something." James admired the bracelet and looked questioningly at Lacey.

"I'll explain it all later," she said. "But it is from a mermaid."

Winston and Glory headed off by themselves while the others took Lily for one last ride. She was getting tired from all the excitement and getting up so early that morning.

"One more ride," said Lacey. "Then it's time to head home."

Lily tried to stifle a yawn as she nodded. "What about the trap race?" she asked.

"That's not for two more hours," said Lacey. "I think we'll miss that, but Glory said she would video record it for us."

After Lily's ride on a 'sea themed' merry-go-round they picked out a dozen donuts and cupcakes and headed for home.

It was close to four o'clock when the trap races actually got started. Winston was the second contestant. He'd pulled off his shirt and shoes and put on a pair of rubber-soled rock climbing shoes. "This year I'm hoping these new shoes will help," he told Glory.

Unfortunately, the shoes didn't help. He made it almost to the end of the row when his foot slipped and he fell into the ocean. He came up sputtering and laughing.

He swam to shore and stepped out of the water where Glory handed him a towel.

"I suppose you got all that on video?" he said wiping his dripping hair.

"I sure did," she said laughing. "I can't wait to show everyone."

####

Because Lacey had been admiring an original watercolor painting on Annette's living room wall, Annette took her to meet some friends of hers who lived in Glen Cove. "This man is a fantastic artist," she told Lacey as she drove. "He made that watercolor painting you keep admiring in my living room."

"The one of the red rose bush beside the white farmhouse door?"

"Yes. And he commissions portraits. I thought he could paint one from the photo you took of Lily with the mermaid."

Lacey smiled. "She would love that."

They pulled into the driveway of a small white house with a view of Clam Cove Beach. A woman peeked out the front window and waved.

After parking they walked to the back porch. Annette hugged the woman with short brown hair as soon as the back door opened.

"Debbie, I'd like you to meet my cousin, Lacey. She's visiting from Arkansas and has been admiring the painting I bought from Chris," said Annette. "I wanted her to see more of his work." Debbie smiled and invited them inside.

Chris had short white hair and a trim white beard and he wore glasses. He was shy about his work and didn't realize how stunning his paintings actually were. His small art studio had paintings of old farmhouses, boats, harbors and landscapes. His portraits included pets as well as people. Debbie showed them photos of several murals he'd painted commercially.

Lacey was so smitten with Chris Merrill's artwork that she bought a small watercolor of flowers and a hummingbird, then asked him to do the painting of Lily. "I'll get you a copy of the photo tomorrow," she promised.

Chris smiled and seemed pleased with her compliments, but Lacey could tell he felt a little overwhelmed by her praise. It was Debbie who displayed his works on a webpage and helped with framing, sales and shipping: Chris just wanted to paint.

"I can't wait to show this to James," said Lacey on the way home. "It's amazing."

## Chapter 22

"Mom, when are we going home?" Lily asked. She was coloring a picture at the kitchen table and her question took Lacey by surprise.

"Are you tired of visiting Maine?" asked Lacey. "I thought you liked going to the beach."

Lily shrugged and looked up from her picture. "I do like the beach, but I miss my horse and all my friends."

Lacey nodded. "I see. Well we were planning to go back right before school started but maybe we should head back sooner."

Lily smiled. "Can we, please?"

James arranged their flights and they left three days later but Michel stayed behind. His college semester didn't start until later in September and that gave him a few more weeks to earn money for school.

Michel said 'goodbye' before he and Winston headed out to check the lobster traps.

Annette shed a few tears when she drove them to the airport. "I'm going to miss all of you," she sniffled. "You have to Facetime me every week."

"I will, promise," said Lacey, giving her a hug. "We've had a wonderful time. Thank you so much for inviting us and letting us stay in your home."

With everyone else gone, Michel moved into the empty spare bedroom. "Hey, it's not like I don't like you sleeping on the top bunk," said Winston. "But you do snore when you're really tired."

Michel rolled his eyes and finished moving his things into the other bedroom. He didn't mention that Winston snored every night.

It was late one afternoon out on the boat when Winston decided he wanted to dive off Damariscove Island again. "I'd like to go down and see if there's anything else of my dad's down there," he told Michel as he put bait into the last lobster trap.

"Could we get Glory to go with us?" asked Michel. "I'm a little nervous about the two of us going out alone. I'm not as experienced as you are."

"I'll ask when she has time off." Winston dropped the trap over the side of the boat with a splash and Michel headed the boat back to the harbor.

Winston called Glory that night.

"I'm sorry Winston, I've got another class I'm required to take for the 'search and rescue team' and it will be every evening after work for the next two weeks. I could go after that," said Glory.

"You're going back to the island?"

"I want to take another look around down there."

"I'm sorry I can't go," she said.

"That's ok, I understand." He was disappointed but he would dive without her.

The next evening the two men took filled tanks with them on the boat. They cut their workday short and headed to the island to dive while there was still light.

The tourists were all gone and the caretaker was in his cabin by the time they reached the island. After suiting up they dropped into the cold water and headed down to the bottom. It took them a few minutes to find the spot where Winston found his dad's swim fin.

After searching through the thick weeds and kelp for twenty minutes they moved a little further away from the boat. Michel pushed through the dark green kelp and brushed his hand carefully over the rocks. Small fish rushed out of the weeds and swam past him brushing his arms and head. When he ducked down to avoid the fish he spotted a huge black area on the other side of the wall of kelp.

Pushing his way through the thick leaves he spotted the mouth of an underwater cave. He backed out and swam over to Winston. He tapped Winston's shoulder and pointed back at the kelp then swam away. Winston immediately followed. Between the two of them they parted the weeds and swam up to the cave opening.

The mouth of the cave looked big enough for a diver to swim through. Winston was about to enter when a huge dark shadow passed overhead. He looked up and found himself staring at the under belly of a nine foot 'great white shark'. He grabbed Michel's arm and pointed up.

Both of them remained motionless as the shark passed overhead. When it was gone they headed back to the boat. No use taking chances with a shark in the area, thought Winston. There'd been a shark attack last year that killed a woman.

When they broke the surface of the water beside the boat, they could see the shark's fin heading toward them. Winston hurried up the ladder and reached down to pull Michel onto the deck. By the time they'd removed their masks the shark was directly behind the boat.

Michel's face turned pale. "That was close. I didn't know there were sharks up here. I thought they didn't like water this cold," he said helping Winston remove his air tank.

"They've become more common in the last few years," said Winston. He removed Michel's tank and they both grabbed a towel. "We'd better wait to check out that cave."

Michel nodded. "Daylight won't last long enough to check out the cave and get back to the boat safely," he said.

"I need to get underwater flashlights for a proper search," added Winston.

When they started the boat engine and the shark swam away from the loud noise. Michel pulled up the anchor and watched the shark's fin disappear.

When Annette heard about what happened she was not happy. "I lost your father out there, please don't let me lose you as well."

"I guess we'll have to get someone else to go with us next time."

"How is that going to help?" she asked with her hands on her hips.

"A third person can be on shark watch," he said.

She shook her head. "I don't like that idea." The oven timer chimed and she turned to pull out the lasagna. "I don't like it at all."

####
Miami, Florida

Cold-water sharks weren't the only threat to humans. According to Jimmy Buffett there are sharks that swim on the land.

Will and Parker had arranged their vacation to Miami. They checked into the Setia Residence Ocean Front Condos on a Thursday afternoon to start their vacation. The Setia boasted three outdoor pools, a sauna, full body massages, free WiFi, cable television, a restaurant, jetted tubs, and a poolside bar. They'd rented a car and went to Bella's Cabaret their first night there.

Bella's advertized itself as the best strip club in south Florida.

A huge six-foot-four bouncer with a trimmed beard and a mean look in his dark eyes welcomed them inside. A pretty hostess seated them at a table near the dance floor. They were on their third round of drinks when a man walked up to their table.

"Well, well, well. Fancy meeting you guys here," said a deep voice.

Will looked up into the cold eyes of Earl Childs. Standing next to him was hulking Sonny Weather. Both of them wore expensive clothes and Earl had a diamond pinky ring on his left hand. They pulled up chairs at Will's table without asking permission and a wave of expensive cologne washed over Will.

"You guys must be doing pretty good to be down here on vacation," said Earl. Although his voice was pleasant, his expression wasn't.

Sonny flexed his muscles and the cartoon tattoos danced on his arms as he leaned on to the top of the table and stared at Parker.

"Yeah, that's right, Earl," said Will hastily. "We're just on vacation. No sence having a pile of money if you can't spend it, right?"

Earl laughed. "You're so right. I'm just wondering if that's the only reason you two guys are here. You're not planning on horning in on my cousin's district, are you?"

"Heck no," said Will, feeling sweat starting to pop out on his forehead. "We like Maine. We got no plans to expand our business."

Earl slapped Will on the back. "That's what I thought. I was just checking." Earl waved one of the strippers over to the table. "Sherry baby, make sure these guys have a good night," he told her. He looked back at Will. "How long you planning to be down here?"

"Just for a week. We're staying at the Setia," said Will nervously.

"Good, that's a nice place," said Earl nodding. "Tomorrow night we've got a little poker game set up in the back room here. You want to join us?"

Will nodded. "Sure thing. What time does it start?" He hoped Earl didn't notice the sweat on his brow.

"Be here by nine o'clock and I'll get you into the back room." Earl stood up and walked away with Sonny following him.

Sherry sat down in the empty seat. She was a buxom bleached blond with tattoos on both arms. She wore a skimpy red dress and stiletto heels. She smiled with bright red lips. "You boys need anything special tonight?" she asked in a sultry voice.

Will, still anxious from his meeting with Earl shook his head. "No, doll, I think we're fine for now. We'll just watch the show. You've got some wicked good dancers in this place," he said wiping the sweat off his forehead.

Sherry got up and kissed Will on the cheek leaving a red blotch of lipstick behind. "OK, whatever you say." She sashayed to the bar and whispered into the ear of a short bald man.

"Why'd you say we wanted to play poker with Earl?" asked a confused Parker.

"I don't know. He took me by surprise," admitted Will.

"I thought we were going to a casino tomorrow night," complained Parker.

"We'll do that tomorrow afternoon after lunch and a massage."

Parker grinned. "OK." He turned his chair to face the dancers and dropped the subject.

Will's stomach felt queasy thinking about playing poker with Earl and his friends. If he won he was worried about what would happen to him. But he didn't want to lose money either. He thought of himself as a pretty good poker player, but it might not be a good idea to win too much money off these guys. Maybe he could throw a few hands so as not to take too much.

Will needn't have worried about winning too much money. By the time he left the club the next night he'd lost over $15,000 to the sharks in Miami.

## Chapter 23
## Maine

Parker was scrutinizing the desserts in the window of a bakery in Rockland when Will grabbed his arm. "Hey, see that woman with the black hair?" said Earl pointing downhill.

Parker looked up and squinted through the sunshine at Glory walking toward the police station. "Yeah, she's pretty. What about her?"

"Isn't she the one who was diving with those two lobster guys last month?" asked Will quickly snapping a photo of Glory with his phone.

"Could be. It's hard to tell from this distance."

"She's wearing a police uniform," hissed Will. "I'll blow up her photo and we'll see if she's the same woman."

"What does it matter?" asked Parker confused. He was still trying to decide which doughnuts he wanted to buy from the bakery.

Will gave an exasperated sigh. "It matters because those two guys were diving off Damariscove Island."

Parker frowned looking up at Will. "So what?"

"Maybe they're watching the island because they know we've been meeting with our suppliers there," said Will. He watched as Glory entered the police station.

Parker's eyes widened. "Oh. You think they're spying on us for the cops?"

Will shrugged. "I don't know. We only meet Earl in the middle of the night."

"Maybe they think we'll get used to seeing them around the island and we won't pay attention when they dive there at night," reasoned Parker.

Will raised his eyebrows. "That's pretty smart thinkin', Parker. You might be right."

Parker grinned. That was the first time Will had ever said he was smart. "Let's get some of these chocolate doughnuts this time," he said pointing at the bakery. "We always get the molasses doughnuts."

"I like the molasses ones," said Will. "We can get both."

Back at his house, Will uploaded the photo of Glory to his computer and enlarged it. After studying it for several minutes he frowned. It was the same woman he saw on the lobster boat diving with the two men. They'd have to keep an eye out for the *Chelsea Two*. He didn't want a couple of dudes to blow his cover. He hadn't worked this area for the last five years to end up in prison.

Parker looked over his shoulder. "It's the same woman, isn't it?"

Will nodded and his eyes took on a mean glint. "If they show up at night, we'll just have to take care of them."

Parker grinned. "Yeah, like we did that other guy who was spying on us."

Will stood up. "Seems like there's always someone trying to poke their nose where it doesn't belong."

"But we took care of the last guy and we made a little extra getting rid of his boat," gloated Parker.

Will smiled and his teeth shone in the lamplight. "We did at that, Parker." He stood up. "Let's go cut that other bag of stuff. A couple dealers sent me emails saying they needed more bags."

They spent the next few hours in the basement mixing baking soda and cocaine. When they finished bagging it, Parker filled his duffle bag.

"Don't get sloppy," warned Will. "Only fifty bags to each guy and watch your back."

Parker gave him a fake salute. "Sure thing, Boss," he laughed before heading upstairs and out to his Camaro.

Will watched Parker drive away. He shook his head. He should have made him take that flashy car back, too. He went into the kitchen to get himself another doughnut.

As he sat at the table he stared at the photo of Glory. She was awfully pretty. It would be a shame to kill her without having a little fun first. He finished off his doughnut and grinned.

## Chapter 24

Glory looked at the data on her computer screen. Another junkie had died over the weekend from what first appeared as an overdose but was actually poisoning. The coroner's report listed rat poison as the cause. She looked over at Officer Adams.

Devon Adams sat with his muscular arms folded over his chest, his eyes closed. She noticed he's recently gotten a haircut. He never let his brown hair get longer than an inch.

"Rough weekend, Devon?" she teased.

He barely opened his brown eyes and squinted at her. "Yeah. I caught the poisoning case and spent fruitless hours going through that junkie's rat's nest of an apartment." Devon was wearing street clothes instead of a uniform today.

She nodded sympathetically. "No clues?"

He shook his head. "Not so much as a decent fingerprint. The place was a pig-sty." He sighed. "It's sad how ordinary, good people fall into the drug trap. Once they get hooked on something their whole life turns to crap." He sat up and looked at her. "Tommy Vince played on the basketball team in high school. He got a scholarship to the University of Southern Maine. Last game of the year he tore the ligaments in his knee and lost everything. Guess that's why he turned to drugs."

"Depression is a horrible thing to go through," commiserated Glory.

Devon shrugged. "I'm sure it is. So the poor guy gets depressed and starts looking for something, anything to make him feel better. The drug dealers zero in on him and that's it. Pretty soon it takes more and more of the stuff to make him forget his pain."

"I know; it's horrible."

"Then when he becomes a liability, the pusher kills him so he can't give information to the police," he said. "So now we have two murders this summer with no clues."

"None at all?" she asked sympathetically.

"Only the fact that both Tommy and Belinda were hooked on cocaine."

"Nothing else? No heroin or Molly? No prescription drugs?"

Devon shook his head. "No signs of anything else in the apartment. Just some contaminated cocaine. The sick bastards poisoned the poor guy."

"Who's working the case with you?" she asked.

"Brent," he said, frowning. "He's a good cop, but he talks too much. Every time I've gone on a stakeout with him I can't get him to shut up. He can talk your ears off."

She laughed. "What does he talk about?"

"What doesn't he talk about is more like it," he laughed. "He's a walking encyclopedia of trivia. You name it and he can talk about it, for hours."

At that moment Officer Brent West walked into the office. "Hi, Glory," he said, walking to Devon's desk.

Brent was the only black man in their small department. He was handsome with dark brown eyes, a strong jaw and black hair. Of average height, he was muscular from working out. His jersey shirt stretched tight across his chest. He knew judo, taekwondo and jiu-jitsu. He could handle just about anyone in a fight.

Both men were wearing civilian clothes today, which meant they were supposed to be undercover. Glory wondered if being undercover in such a small community meant anything. She figured the residents knew all the police officers. Maybe it was to fool all the tourists and out-of-town crooks.

"Adams, we're supposed to go talk to Micky."

Devon glanced at his watch. "Sorry, I forgot." He stood up and the two of them left.

They found Micky Stearns standing on a street corner in Camden. Even though it was summer he wore a long sleeve jacket and knit cap over long greasy blond hair. He spotted the officers as they pulled their unmarked police car up to the curb. He turned and slowly walked into the dark alley between a candy store and a tourist trap selling t-shirts.

The two cops followed him. "Hi, Micky," said Officer Adams. "Kinda warm to be wearing a coat, isn't it?"

"Hey, I'm always cold," said Micky. "The wind off the ocean ain't warm." Micky was skinny and pale. He had dark circles under both eyes and his hands shook so much he usually kept them tucked in his pockets. "I heard something on the street you should know about."

"Yeah, what did you hear?" asked Officer West.

Mickey stuck out his right hand. "You know what I charge."

Brent handed him two twenties. "Ok, what have you heard?"

"Two guys from New York brought in the last shipment of coke," he said, stuffing the bills in a coat pocket. "It was so strong it had to be cut a second time. They meet each other out off one of the islands down by Boothbay."

"Do you know who the main suppliers are in town?" asked Devon.

"I only know my dealer. And he's small potatoes." Micky shook his head. "All I know's that they moved up here from New Hampshire a couple of years ago. That's when all the junkies switched from heroin and Molly to coke. These suppliers were smart. They offered coke at reduced prices until everyone was hooked, then they jacked up the price."

Devon and Brent knew Micky was a user and he was beginning to look pretty bad. Brent patted Micky's shoulder.

"Micky, you need to go to rehab and get off this stuff. It's going to kill you," said Brent.

Micky shrugged and hung his head. "I know, but it's the only thing that helps me forget." Micky turned and walked back out onto the street.

Back in the car Devon turned to Brent. "What's the story with Micky?"

Brent sighed. "Four years ago Micky was smoking a joint and fell asleep. He caused a fire that burnt up his small houseboat and killed his girlfriend. He's never gotten over it."

Devon started the car and shook his head. "If his dealer finds out he was talking to us, he'd be the next rat poison death."

Brent looked out the window. "I know," he said softly.

## Chapter 25

"What are you doing down here in the basement, Mom?" asked Winston from the basement doorway.

Annette stepped back from the pile of boxes she was sorting through. She brushed a lock of hair off her forehead and wiped her hands down the sides of the old pair of jeans she wore. "I've finally decided to go through your father's boxes. Do you want to help?"

Winston climbed down the stairs and pulled the cord to turn on another overhead light. "How can you see anything down here with half the lights off?" He walked over to the corner of the room and hugged her. The basement also served as the laundry room and he could hear the dryer running. "You've been busy this morning," he said.

"Where's Michel?" she asked, pulling men's clothing from a box.

"He's in the kitchen eating his third bowl of cereal. I think I've finally found someone who can eat more than me," he laughed.

Annette folded the clothes and put them back in the box. "Could you stack this box over by the stairs with the others?"

"Sure." He took the box from her and set it on top of another one by the side of the stairs. "What are you going to do with them?"

She wiped her cheek and left a dusty streak across it. "The Boys and Girls Club is having a rummage sale and I offered to donate some things. Most of your dad's clothes are in good shape and I found a new pair of deck shoes still in the box."

Winston nodded. "That's a good charity. Dad would approve." He watched as she opened another box then quickly closed it again. "What's in that box?"

"It's stuff from his office," she said. "Do you want to go through it before I toss it out? I've only got one other box to look through. Take out anything important; the rest can go in the trash. I've stacked the things we need to throw away over by the washer."

"I'll go through it, but I'm taking it upstairs where the light's better."

He carried the box upstairs to the living room and set it on the coffee table. He opened the lid and peered inside. A notebook, pens and pencils, a roll of almost empty scotch tape and a twelve-inch ruler were scattered on top of the other items in the box. He pulled them out and dug deeper. Several labeled CD's were bound together with a rubber band. The label said they contained family photos from the last ten years. He set those aside to save. An old TV remote that was no longer useful, a box of white envelopes and a plastic container of paper clips were in the next layer. Some receipts for bait and supplies for the boat were several years old and now useless.

In the very bottom of the box was a used spiral notebook. The pages were wrinkled on the edges. He opened the book. Seeing his father's handwriting brought a lump to his throat.

Michel walked up and looked over his shoulder. "What's all this stuff?"

"Things from my dad's desk," said Winston.

The two of them looked at the writing on the first page. In big letters Richard had written. *Dixce Bull*. Underneath were historical facts about the life of the pirate. The next pages held a list of the different ships he'd robbed and the facts about the pillaging and burning of the trading station in Pemaquid.

"This looks like the research Dad was doing about that pirate Dixce Bull I told you about," said Winston. "I didn't know he'd dug up all of this information."

"Looks like this pirate caused a lot of trouble," said Michel.

Winston nodded. "But according to legend he was only in Maine for a year or two." Winston scanned a few pages. The next section of research contained drawings of Damariscove Island and Cushing Island in Casco Bay.

"He did some research about the water levels around the two islands where there might be buried treasure," said Winston pointing to the drawings.

"Did your father really believe those legends?" asked Michel. "Has anyone ever found any buried treasure around here?"

Winston looked up from the drawings. "We're not sure. In 1855, a rum pot full of gold coins was plowed up by a farmer on Richmond Island and according to history the dates of the coins fit with the Dixce Bull stories. But no one could prove it. Some people thought the farmer who owned the land earlier buried the coins."

Michel nodded. "What else does your dad have written about the pirate treasure? What would it be worth?"

"He didn't write anything about that," said Winston. "But look at this drawing of Damariscove Island." He pointed to the outline of the island's beach. "Back in the sixteen hundreds when the pirates were here, the island was much bigger."

"What are those black blotches on the sketch?"

Winston pulled the drawing closer to read some smudged ink by one of the black blotches. "It looks like it says 'cave' right here." He pointed to the writing.

"Let's get a recent map of the island and see if one of those spots is where we saw the opening to the underwater cave last time we went diving," suggested Michel.

Winston hurried to the small back room where his father's office had been. On the shelves were books with nautical maps. "Dad was always trying to find neat places for us to dive so he kept all these maps."

Michel pulled a book off the shelf. The title was *Shipwrecks of Maine.* He thumbed through the pages. "There must be hundreds of ships that wrecked off the coast of Maine," he said in awe. "This book says there are over 3,500 miles of coastline in Maine counting the islands. It lists the names of seventy-five wrecks and says that's not all of them."

"Yeah, Dad and I dived to a couple of them," said Winston absentmindedly. He was turning the pages in a big book of maps looking for Damariscove Island. When he found it he opened the book on the desk to compare with the drawing.

Still reading the book about shipwrecks, Michel learned that some of the ships had broken up completely, some had been raised and others ruined by scavengers. But there were still quite a few that would make good dives.

Winston pointed to the map that showed where the first settlers built on the island. One of the buildings was now used as the caretaker's cottage. "This gives us a reference point even though the coastline has changed so much," he said pointing to the cottage on his father's drawing.

"It looks like this cave is the same one you found underwater." Winston pointed to the cave on the east side of the island shown in the book. "The same one my dad must have been diving to when he disappeared."

"We have to go back out there," said Michel.

## Chapter 26
## Arkansas

"Come in, Mr. Ford," she said, opening the front door wider. "Thank you so much for taking my case." Wanda Fist was a short, plump woman with brown hair and hazel eyes. She looked tired and her curly hair was escaping the bun on the back of her head. She wore a printed blouse and black slacks.

"Please, call me James," he said as he walked inside and closed the door behind him. The sound of children's voices floated into the house from the backyard. She led him into the living room where he had to step over children's toys on the floor to reach the couch.

"Excuse the mess," she said wearily. "I have three foster children under the age of five and I can't seem to keep up with them." She began picking up toys and tossing them into a plastic clothes' basket set against the wall. He waited for her to finish.

"Can I offer you something to drink? Juice or coffee?" she asked.

"No, I'm fine. Please sit down and tell me more about your son, Jonathan."

She sat down on a worn lounge chair across from him and handed him a photo. "That was taken shortly before he went missing," she said. "He's eighteen now and the police figure he ran away and as an adult they won't look for him unless foul play is involved." She gave a weary sigh. "He might have run away. I've asked a lot of him since his father died." Tears formed in her eyes and she brushed away one that escaped down her cheek.

James nodded and looked at the photo. A pleasant looking young man with brown hair and eyes wearing black-rimmed glasses smiled out from the picture. "When did your husband pass away?" he asked.

"Three years ago. Jonathan was with him in the car. Arthur was killed instantly according to the coroner. Jonathan had a severely broken leg, a compound fracture, and a concussion. He spent four weeks in the hospital in traction. They managed to fix his leg but now he walks with a limp. We got a settlement from the truck that hit them, but it doesn't replace my husband." Sorrow radiated from her eyes. "I lost my husband, now I've lost my son." She began crying in earnest and wiped angrily at the tears.

James handed her a box of tissues from the small table next to the couch.

She wiped her face and blew her nose. "I started taking in foster children two years ago. The house was too quiet with Jonathan in school all day. It helps a little to have children around." She forced a smile. "I didn't realize Jonathan was so unhappy."

"You haven't heard anything from him at all?" asked James.

She shook her head. "He graduated from high school last May. He went missing a week later. He should be starting school at the University of Arkansas in two weeks. I thought he was excited to go to college, but maybe not."

"Tell me a little more about him," said James. "Did he seem upset or depressed at all?"

"Not that I could tell. Jonathan's a good kid. He's smart, all A's in accelerated classes in high school. He tested out of three freshman courses at the college. Never took drugs or drank alcohol. I don't know why he would have just run away," she said. "I'm worried something has happened to him and the police won't listen to me."

James nodded sympathetically. "What about his friends?"

She took a deep breath. "He doesn't have many. He's always been a little shy and didn't fit in with the jocks or popular kids at school. The only after school club he enjoyed was a computer class," she explained. "His best friend is Pauly, a boy who lives next door."

"Did the police talk to Pauly?"

She shook her head. "No. Paul Trent has Down's syndrome. He's kind of slow and his speech is difficult to understand. He's only fifteen. The police never even interviewed him. Jonathan was the only one who seemed to connect with Pauly. He used to take him to the park or to the movies and he taught him to play video games."

"Do you think his parents would let me speak to Pauly?"

"I'm sure they would. I'll give them a call." She pulled her phone out of her pocket and asked Sheila Trent if she would bring Pauly over to talk to the detective she'd hired.

A few minutes later Sheila knocked on the door.

Pauly was short with the classic facial features of Down's syndrome. His slanted eyes and low set ears were the most noticeable features. He wore clean sweat pants, a t-shirt and sneakers. He smiled when he saw Wanda and gave her a hug.

"Pauly said he'd be happy to talk to someone trying to find Jonathan," said Sheila.

Pauly walked up to James with a big grin on his face. He sat down on the couch and looked up at James. "You gonna find Jon?" he asked. His voice was soft and low, almost a mumble, but James understood him.

James smiled. "I'm going to try my best to find him."

Pauly nodded.

"Did Jonathan say anything to you about leaving home?" asked James looking directly in the boy's eyes. "This is very important Pauly."

Pauly looked at the floor. "Secret," he whispered.

James looked startled. "He told you a secret?"

Pauly pinched his lips closed.

"This is very, very important, Pauly. Jonathan might be in trouble," coaxed James. "You can whisper the secret in my ear."

Pauly smiled and moved closer to James who leaned down to the boy.

Pauly's lips touched James' ear. "Jon ran away to circus."

James looked puzzled. "He told you this?"

Pauly nodded. "Pretty girl there."

James looked at Wanda. "Was there a circus in town the week Jonathan disappeared?"

"I don't think so," she said.

Sheila's eyes widened. "Jonathan took Pauly to the carnival that week. In fact they went three times. Pauly was sad when the carnival left town."

"Do you know the name of the carnival?"

She shook her head. "No idea. But Pauly had fun and Jonathan seemed eager to take him. Is that important?"

"It could be. Thank you both," said James patting Pauly's shoulder. "You've been a big help. Have a nice day."

Pauly looked at Wanda. "I miss Jon." He frowned.

Sheila took Pauly's hand. "Let's go home. You can help me make cookies." Pauly grinned and they left.

"What was that about?" asked Wanda.

"Pauly said Jonathan ran away to the circus because of a pretty girl."

Wanda put her hand to her mouth. "Oh my gosh, I remember something. A few days before he left Jonathan asked me for $1900 to help a friend. He wouldn't give me a reason or tell me who the friend was. I told him I needed more information." She looked upset. "I should have given it to him."

"Not necessarily. It could have been a scam," reassured James. "I'll find out which carnival was in the area in May and check it out." He stood up. "I'll be back in touch."

####

Lacey used her computer skills to try and find the carnival. "There's a website called CarnivalWarehouse.com that lists all the carnivals in the United States and their schedules. I'll see which one was in this area in May," she told James.

"How do you know that?" he asked.

She grinned. "I'm a computer genius."

He leaned over and gave her a kiss, then watched as her fingers flew over the keyboard. The site popped up and she scrolled down the list.

"I had no idea there were so many carnivals still around," he said looking at the list.

"This one looks promising," she pointed to the computer screen. The *Tally Shows* carnival out of Fort Worth, Texas was at the Bentonville County Fairgrounds for two weeks in May. "It's in Tulsa, Oklahoma this week."

"That's only a two hour drive from here," said James looking at the address. "I'll head over there and see what I can find out. It's a slim lead, but all I've got."

"Stay safe," she said, giving him a kiss.

"Always."

Ever one to be careful, James took put his revolver in the shoulder holster under his shirt. Things could go wrong too easily to leave it behind. He made it to Tulsa by two o'clock and parked in the lot beside the carnival site. Because it was a Saturday the rides were open and there was a line of people buying tickets. James waited his turn and bought a ticket.

Inside the gates lively music was playing. Mixed smells assaulted his nose immediately. Hot dogs, burgers, funnel cakes, and popcorn enticed the crowds from all sides. Hoots and hollers floated through the air from the various rides. He walked past the Ferris wheel and roller coaster as he looked for the carneys' trailers. Lily would have loved some of the rides. She was a daredevil and would have been thrilled by the Cliff Hanger, Kamikaze and Starship rides that swooped, dropped and swirled around frantically.

He'd reached the area where games of skill were offered when he spotted a young man working the shooting gallery who looked remarkably like Jonathan. The boy waved at him and hollered.

"Try your luck, Mister? Only five dollars! You could win a stuffed bear for your sweetheart!" yelled Jonathan with a grin.

James sauntered over and handed the boy five dollars. He picked up a rifle and fired at the target. The pellet veered to the left. He corrected for the obvious slant in the sight and hit the bull's eye seven times.

"Way to go, Mister. Pick out something from the first row." The first row held three-inch tall stuffed bears probably worth a dollar.

"How do you win one of those?" asked James pointing to the thirty-six inch bears hanging from the ceiling.

"You have to pay twenty dollars and hit the bull's eye on ten targets," said Jonathan.

James handed him a twenty and proceeded to take out all the targets strung up on the back of the booth.

Jonathan's mouth fell open.

"I'll take that big pink one," said James knowing Lily would love it.

Jonathan reluctantly climbed on a small ladder and unhooked the bear. "Here you go, sir. You're a great shot."

Just as James received the bear, a tall muscular man walked up and scowled at Jonathan.

James walked away from the booth and pretended to study the next game in the row of booths as he listened to the conversation behind him.

"Jon, you're a lousy carnie. No one, I repeat no one is supposed to win one of the big bears," growled the man.

"I know, Jeremy," said Jonathan cringing. "But he won it fair and square."

Jeremy opened a side door and entered the booth. He picked up the gun James had used and adjusted the sight on the barrel. "You have to make it so they can't win much."

James stepped back in front of the shooting gallery. "He didn't know I used to be a cop. I figured out how it worked," said James staring at Jeremy. "I don't think your customers would like what you do to the sights."

Jeremy glared at James. He had tattoos running up to his neck on both muscular arms. He wore a muscle shirt to show off his arms and it stretched tightly across his chest. His black hair was spiked up and he wore a diamond ear stud in his right ear. "Mind your own business, mister," he growled.

James turned to the boy. "Are you Jonathan Fisk?"

Jonathan's eyes widened and he nodded.

"Who wants to know?" snarled Jeremy.

"I'm a private detective sent to find Jonathan. Name's James Ford."

Jeremy squinted at him with a hateful look, but he left the booth and stalked away.

"Jonathan, your mother is worried about you," said James.

Jonathan hung his head. "I should have called her." He looked up at James and his jaw tightened. "But I knew she wouldn't understand and would tell me to come home."

"Do you like working here?" asked James looking around.

"Not really."

"Then why stay?"

"Because of Susie." Jonathan called to a carnie walking by and asked him to mind the booth. He led James to the back of the lot and opened the door to a small trailer.

"I've been staying here with Susie Quaint. I met her in May and I started working here to help pay off a debt she owes Jeremy," explained Jonathan.

"That's why you asked your mother for $1900?"

He nodded. "I'm working here for free so my money can be applied to Susie's debt."

"You still haven't paid it off after three months?" asked James incredulously.

"They deduct my food and our rent and expenses from my pay."

"What other expenses do you have?"

"If someone wins a big bear, I have to cover its cost of thirty five dollars," he admitted. "I'm not very good at this."

"How much do you and Susie still owe Jeremy?" asked James.

"About $900."

"At this rate you'll be here until Christmas," warned James.

"I know."

The trailer door opened and a young woman walked in. Susie looked at Jonathan in surprise. "Who's this?" she asked, upset. "You're not supposed to bring customers to my trailer."

Susie was a pretty young woman with blond hair and blue eyes. She was thin and wore a pair of skin-tight jeans and a halter top. James thought she looked about nineteen.

Jonathan introduced James. "Susie, this is James. My mom sent him."

Susie turned to run away, but James grabbed her arm and forced her to face them.

"This is a scam, isn't it, Susie?" asked James. "How old are you?"

Susie blanched. "I'm twenty-six."

Jonathan looked askance. "You're scamming me? You told me you were nineteen."

Susie rolled her eyes. "I get guys to work for free to cover a fake debt."

James let go of her arm and she crossed them across her chest. "Last guy was here for six months before he figured it out," she said proudly.

Jonathan's face turned red. "You bitch! No wonder you didn't want to be my girlfriend."

Susie's chin came up. "I'm not a whore. I don't sleep with my mark."

James sighed. "Jonathan, get your things. We're going home."

It took Jonathan ten minutes to gather his meager clothing and personal items. When they were in the SUV headed back to Arkansas, Jonathan looked at James.

"I feel like an idiot. I can't believe I fell for her scam," he complained.

"Hey, even smart guys can be scammed by a pretty face," commiserated James.

## Chapter 27
## Maine

Glory convinced Winston to wait to go diving until she could go with them. Michel only had two weeks left before his college started in Arkansas. That meant they ended up having to go out one evening after she got off work and Winston had emptied his traps. They were all tired but excited to see what might be in the underwater cave.

Tourist season was over for the year on Damariscove Island and the caretaker had closed up the cabin and gone back to the mainland. The only residents now were the wildlife. Seagulls swooped overhead making their noisy cries when Winston dropped anchor off the east coast of the island. A few sleepy seals rested on the rocks by the surf. He noticed an expensive speedboat anchored further out from the island but didn't pay any attention to it.

"We still have a couple of hours before it gets dark," said Glory optimistically. "We have plenty of time to dive but we'll be heading home in the dark."

Winston scanned the sky. "I don't like the looks of those dark clouds," he said, scanning the sky south of them. He turned all the boat's night-time running lights on to make certain anyone traveling in the area would see it. No sence causing an accident.

Winston scanned the area for any signs of sharks but didn't see any.

They hurriedly got into their dry-suits and helped each other with the tanks. One by one they dropped into the water and headed down to the area where Michel found the cave.

####

Will lowered his binoculars. "I knew if we waited long enough they'd eventually show up at night. That woman cop is with them. Damn it. If they think we don't know they're spying on us, they're dumber than a fence post."

Parker laughed. "That's funny, Will. Dumber than a fence post."

Will glared at him and Parker shut up.

"There's no other reason for divers to be out here this late in the evening," griped Will. "It will be dark in a few hours."

"Maybe sooner if those clouds mean a storm is coming. Think those guys are undercover cops?" asked Parker.

Will shrugged and tucked the binoculars under his seat.

"Whatcha gonna do about them?"

"I don't know. Let me think about it." Will scowled at the empty lobster boat.

"Bet you'll come up with a good plan," encouraged Parker.

Will sat down and sipped his beer. He wasn't about to let a couple of undercover cops get away with ruining a business he'd worked so hard on.

####

Down underwater Michel led the way to the cave opening. A school of tiny mackerel swam over his head as he groped through the sea grass. The cave eluded him for a few minutes but he finally pushed aside enough kelp to see it again. He waved to the others and swam through the plants toward the cave.

Winston insisted on going inside first. He figured if he could fit through the opening the others wouldn't have a problem. He turned on his underwater flashlight and ducked his head into the dark mouth of the cave.

It was the peak of high tide and there was no current to fight against. He kept his head tucked down and his legs straight behind him to avoid bumping into the jagged rocks along the top of the tunnel. Barnacles and sea plants clung to the walls around him. Tiny fish darted through the beam of his flashlight.

Glory entered behind Winston shining her flashlight toward his swim fins ahead of her. After pushing aside the kelp Michel brought up the rear. The temperature of the water got colder as they swam deeper inside. The tunnel remained fairly straight for about fifty feet then took a slight turn upward. Winston twisted his body to make the turn and after three kicks of his fins his head broke out of the pool of water.

Winston swam forward until his feet met the floor of the cave. Raising his flashlight he looked above his head to see how much room he had before attempting to stand up. He needn't have worried. The ceiling was ten feet above him. The cave was big, the light barely reaching the ceiling, which was covered with short stalactites. Glory popped up beside him shortly followed by Michel. The three of them removed their masks.

The air in the cave was cold and dank, smelling of salt water and dead plants. Luminescent rocks shone back at them when a beam of light touched the walls ahead.

Glory pointed to the edge of the water line on the floor. "It will be slippery with all that algae. Be careful," she warned.

Winston stepped out of the water onto the sand and rocks. Even though it was high tide, this part of the cave was dry and probably never got very wet. Glory walked up beside him and took off her fins.

"I can't walk in this gear," she complained. Winston helped her remove her tank.

They left their fins and tanks in a pile on the cave floor before heading deeper inside. The sand and rocks were cold on their bare feet.

Their combined flashlight beams lit up the area where they stood but didn't reach the far wall at the back of the cave. The cave was at least sixty feet deep and about twenty feet wide. Winston swung his flashlight beam back and forth as he moved forward leading the way. He jumped when the beam disturbed several big hermit crabs that scurried back toward the water.

"Looks like hermit crabs live in here," he said over his shoulder. His voice sounded eerie echoing off the cold walls.

The others followed quietly scanning the floor to avoid small stalagmites and sharp rocks. At one point, Winston stubbed his toe and softly yelped. The sound echoed overhead.

"Watch out," he warned. "The floor's rough."

Near the back wall stalagmites grew up from the floor two feet high. As Winston's light swept over them it picked up something piled against the back wall. Moving closer his light caught the flash of blue. Walking closer the beam picked up something white. When Glory added her light to his, a bony skull stared back at them.

"What's that?" asked Michel walking up beside Winston.

Glory swept her light over the scene. "It's a dead body." She stepped ahead of the men and leaned over the corpse. "It looks like a man still wearing a dry-suit." Her eyes widened and she turned to Winston.

He moved closer to look at the body. Hermit crabs had removed the flesh from the face and hands but there was still a bit of short, dark red hair attached to the skull. "I think that's my father," he said with a shaky voice. He took a step back and bumped into Michel.

"Don't touch anything," warned Glory.

They shined their lights on the body as she examined it. On the left leg of the blue dry-suit there was a suspicious small round whole. Glory examined it closely and turned to Winston. "It looks like he was shot," she said softly. "He must have crawled in here to hide and bled to death. I'm so sorry, Winston."

"So it was probably a bullet hole in his swim fin," observed Michel.

Winston nodded then his eyes widened. "Look on the wall beside him." He pointed to some faint writing on the cave's dark rock wall.

They pointed their lights at the writing. It appeared to have been scratched on the wall with a piece of broken seashell.

Peering closer Winston gasped. The writing was faint but readable. It said, *"Tell wife + son love them. Richard"*

Winston reached out and touched the writing. "It is my dad," he acknowledged.

Michel patted his shoulder in sympathy.

"We need to leave him and go report this to the authorities," said Glory. "They'll want to send a Crime Scene Team down here."

"I kind of hate to leave him alone," said Winston.

"I'll go radio it in," volunteered Michel.

"I'd better come with you," said Glory. "I can tell them exactly where we are. They'll send someone out from the Coast Guard."

"I'll come back here after I make the call," said Michel handing Winston his flashlight. "In case yours runs out of batteries."

Winston nodded thanks and sat down on the floor of the cave beside his father.

After Michel helped Glory put on her tank, she led the way out of the cave. Michel followed closely to make use of her light. When they reached the surface and came up out of the water they noticed a speedboat floating beside Winston's boat.

They swam to the lobster boat and climbed onboard. It was dark and only a sliver of moonlight lit up the deck. Storm clouds moved overhead but it hadn't started to rain. The clouds blocked most of the moonlight and the running lights didn't illuminate the inside of the wheelhouse cabin. They were taken completely by surprise as they were removing their tanks, when a voice from the wheelhouse called out to them.

"It's about time you came back up."

Startled, they turned around to see a man pointing a revolver at them. A second man stepped forward. The man with the revolver had brown hair pulled back into a ponytail. The second man had short blond hair.

"Pretending to go diving while you spy on us didn't turn out to be such a good idea, did it?" asked Will. He waved his gun at them. "Sit down on the deck," he ordered.

"We don't know what you're talking about," said Michel.

"Who are you?" demanded Glory.

Parker stepped forward and slapped Glory in the face. It wasn't a vicious slap but it left a red mark on her cheek. She glared at him.

"He said sit down!" ordered Parker.

They reluctantly sat down on the deck.

"I'll be asking the questions," said Will. "Where's the other guy?"

Both of them remained silent. After a few seconds, Will moved closer to Glory and pointed the revolver at her head.

"I said, where's the other guy?" demanded Will, touching the barrel tip to her forehead.

"He's still down there," said Michel hurriedly. "We found his father and he wanted to stay with the body while we radioed for help."

"Don't tell them anything," hissed Glory. She desperately wanted to take out these two but she was worried Michel would get hurt.

Will stepped back and waved the gun at her. "You're the cop, right? You're the one spying. You might want to be more cooperative."

"Look, you guys, we aren't spying on anyone. We don't have any idea what you're talking about," said Michel, hoping to convince them. "We've been looking for Winston's father."

Parker's eyes widened. He turned and looked at Will. "They were looking for that diver," he said. "They don't know about the drugs."

"Shut up, Parker, you idiot."

"What do you know about Richard Prescott?" asked Glory. "Did you shoot him?"

Will ignored her. "We'll have to take them with us," he told Parker.

#####

Winston wondered what was taking so long. Michel should've been back by now. He grudgingly left his father to go see what was taking so long.

As he approached the surface of the water it was dark. But there were too many boat running lights shining on the surface for them to be from his boat alone. He wondered if a Coast Guard vessel was in the area and had already gotten here.

When his head broke the surface he saw it wasn't a Coast Guard boat. It was a speedboat floating right next to his boat. Two men were attempting to drag Michel and Glory on to the other boat. He ducked down and kicked his way to the back of his boat.

Michel fought with Parker until he pulled a gun and bashed him in the side of the head with the butt of the revolver. Michel collapsed against Parker who was barely able to push him onto the other boat. Michel landed in a heap on the deck.

By the time Winston pulled himself up the boat ladder Michel had been dropped onto the speedboat and both men were struggling with Glory. She punched and kicked at the two men while they yelled obscenities at her.

"Stop fighting," said Parker. "We just want to talk."

Glory landed a punch to the side of Parker's face and he yelped, losing his footing. He fell backwards onto Will's boat.

Winston stepped onto the boat deck. Neither men noticed him until he threw his mask at Will and hit him in the face. He cursed and let go of Glory's arm.

Will looked up to see Winston barreling down on him. Parker stood up on the speedboat and stared at Winston. While Will fought with Glory, Parker started the engine, pulled the rope line free that held the boats together and screamed at Will.

"Get on the boat! Leave her!" Parker was having trouble keeping the boats close together.

Will saw his boat floating away and decided to forget about the woman. He turned, gave a flying leap and jumped into his boat, crashing to the floor. Parker jammed the boat in gear and they sped away with Michel.

Glory hurriedly radioed the Coast Guard while Winston pulled up the boat's anchor. By the time Winston got his boat started and turned around, the speedboat had disappeared in the darkness. At that moment the storm clouds burst and rain poured down in torrents.

The distant sound of the speedboat faded and it would be impossible to follow them.

Chapter 28
Arkansas

"Lacey? It's Annette. I know it's late but I needed to call and tell you something horrible has happened."

"Let me put this on speaker phone so James can hear, too," said Lacey waving for James to come listen to the call. "What's going on, Annette?"

"Winston's boat was attacked tonight and some pretty shady characters that we think are drug dealers kidnapped Michel," she said breathlessly. "I'm so sorry. The police are already involved but James might want to come up here."

"Tell us what happened," said James.

"I'll let Winston tell you." She handed the phone to her son.

"Glory, Michel and I were out diving in that place where we found my dad's swim fin. Michel had found the entrance to a cave and we'd seen some of dad's notes so we knew he was hunting for pirate treasure in that area. Sorry, I'm getting off subject," said Winston. "Anyway, we found my dad's body in the cave. He'd been shot. When Michel and Glory went to radio the Coast Guard there were two men on my boat. They accused us of spying on them. They're drug smugglers. Anyway they tried to take Glory and Michel on to their boat at gunpoint. I surfaced in time to help Glory, but they took Michel."

"Oh no!" said Lacey. She looked helplessly at James as tears sprang to her eyes.

"What are the police doing to find him?" asked James.

"Glory has a pretty good description of their speedboat and they were stupid enough to call each other by their first names. The Coast Guard is searching for the boat and the police are researching the names. But I figured you'd want to come help."

"You're right on that. I'll book a flight right away," said James.

"I have to go," said Winston. "The police are here and have more questions." He ended the call.

James pulled Lacey into a hug. "Try not to worry. I'll pack and try to catch the red-eye flight. He's a tough kid and he's smart," he said trying to give her hope that everything would turn our all right.

"You let me know everything as soon as you get there," she said, pulling his suitcase out of the closet. "I want to come with you, but I know I'd only get in your way."

He kissed her and started putting clothes in the case.

####

Michel slowly regained consciousness. His head was pounding and he felt dizzy when he opened his eyes. Shutting his eyes, he tried to make sense of where he was. He was lying on his side on a wooden floor. The floor gently moved side to side and he could hear water lapping close by. He tried to move his arms but they were tied together behind his back. His legs were tied together at the ankles.

He opened his eyes again and the dizziness seemed to lessen. There was dim light coming through a small window over his head and he could see he was in a wooden boathouse. He was tucked against the wall of a wooden fishing boat. He managed to push himself into a sitting position which made his head throb. He looked around and saw the speedboat parked next to the boat he was sitting on. The boathouse door was closed but there was enough light to tell it was early morning.

He shifted his legs to get more comfortable then began searching for something to use to cut through his ropes. There were tools, ropes, fishing gear and fuel containers in the boathouse but he couldn't get to anything. He searched the area where he sat and spotted a cabinet door. Scooting himself across the boat deck he managed to reach the cabinet. When he opened it he was disappointed to see a bait bucket and cooler. No tools.

Behind him was the wheelhouse cabin. He began scooting toward it hoping to find something sharp enough to cut rope. It took a few minutes to get to the open cabin. He pushed his back against the wall and managed to use his legs to push himself upright. He hopped inside. Unfortunately none of the drawers held a knife, but he did find an old glass bottle with a little dark liquid in the bottom. Turning his back he used his hands to pick up the bottle. He threw it to the floor and was rewarded by the sound of breaking glass.

He sat down on the floor and scooted back toward the broken glass bottle. He managed to pick up a shard and was able to maneuver it with his fingers to begin sawing at the rope around his wrists. It was slow going and he cut his wrist at one point but he kept at it. He'd just managed to cut though one rope and felt it loosen as the door to the boathouse was pushed open.

Parker looked into the boat. "Where is he?" he barked.

Will pointed to the wheelhouse. "He woke up and moved over there."

Michel frantically pulled at the rope but was unable to get both hands free.

Parker walked over to him and spotted the broken bottle. "Thought you'd get free, did you?" he laughed. He reached down to grab Michel by the arm just as Michel managed to free his right hand. He swung at Parker as hard as he could with the shard of glass. He managed to cut Parker's forearm causing him to jump back screaming. Blood poured down his arm and dripped off Parker's fingers onto the floor.

"Why you bastard!" yelled Parker grabbing his arm to stop the bleeding. He kicked Michel in the ribs causing him to fall over.

Will walked up and pointed his gun at Michel. "Enough of that!" he yelled.

Grabbing Michel by the hair he pulled sideways enough to see that only one hand was still tied. He stomped on Michel's free hand shattering the glass shard into pieces that pierced Michel's palm.

Michel grunted in pain and gritted his teeth. He wouldn't let them know how much that hurt. It felt like his fingers were broken as well as bleeding.

Will threw Parker a dirty piece of towel. Cover that up and go back inside. Bandage it and get back out here.

Parker nodded, his face pale as he wrapped his arm and climbed off the boat.

Will looked down at Michel. "You're more trouble than you're worth." He kicked him in the side of the head knocking him unconscious.

While Michel lay still, Will retied both hands. He looked in disgust at the blood on the floor of his boat. He wrapped another piece of rag around Michel's hand to keep it from making more mess. He sat down in a deck chair to decide what to do with this troublemaker. He would eventually get rid of him, but he wanted some answers first.

####

James' red-eye flight took him to the Atlanta airport. He arrived at three o'clock and had a mere twenty-minute layover. Just barely enough time to get to the next gate. The flight to Portland was already boarding when he rushed up.

He landed in Portland, Maine at seven o'clock. He managed to get a rental car and leave the airport by seven-thirty. Another ninety minutes would get him to Rockland.

He'd phoned ahead and Glory was waiting for him at the Prescott's house in Thomaston. After phoning Lacey to let her know he'd arrived safely, he sat down in the living room to hear Glory's update. She explained in detail about what happened on the boat.

"The police were contacted by the DEA when they began searching for a 'Will' and 'Parker' involved in drugs. Seems there's been an agent in the area investigating them we didn't know about," said Glory. "They're putting together a SWAT team with our men and theirs. They plan to hit William Furman's house in thirty minutes. I figured you'd want to be there."

"I sure do. I'll need a weapon," said James.

Glory frowned. "I'm sorry I can't legally give you one."

Winston spoke up. "I have a pistol that was my dad's. You can use it."

He took James back to his father's office and opened a desk drawer. He handed James a 'Smith and Wesson .380 ACP' semi-automatic pistol and a box of cartridges. "Dad got this after we had a break-in on his boat three years ago."

James loaded the pistol and took the spare magazine. "Thanks."

"I'm sorry this happened. I feel like it's my fault," said Winston.

James shook his head. "Of course it's not your fault. You had no idea these idiots suspected you of spying on them."

Winston nodded. "I know. Just get him back. He's like a brother to me."

James patted his shoulder. "That's what I plan to do."

## Chapter 29
## Maine

Will's house showed no signs of life when the SWAT team arrived. They left the van two houses down the street and silently surrounded the place. James and Glory were suited up with bulletproof vests and instructions to stay in the van until the 'all clear' signal was given.

James chafed at the restriction. "Can't we at least stand outside?" he whispered to Glory.

She nodded and opened the back door. They walked around the van and watched as the team busted through the front door of Will's house. It only took five minutes for the leader to exit the house. He stood on the front porch with a frustrated expression on his face as he waved at Glory to come over.

"The house is empty," Officer Brock Hamilton admitted. "They were here earlier because the coffee pot is still warm. Damn it!" In frustration he cracked his knuckles and silently cursed.

Brock Hamilton was in his forties and a veteran of the DEA. Today he was heading up the SWAT team. Originally from Australia, he spoke with a trace of an accent. He removed his helmet and brushed back his black hair. Tall and muscular, Officer Hamilton was a force to be reckoned with. He glared at the house and rubbed his jaw as if it had foiled him.

A member of his team tapped Brock on the shoulder. "There's blood in the bathroom," he said before leading them into the house. He pointed to the bathroom sink where streaks of blood ran down the bowl and bandage wrapping papers were crumpled on the floor.

"If someone used those small bandages it couldn't be too bad," said Brock.

James knew Brock was trying to make light of the blood to make him feel better. Glory and James left the team to finish checking the house and went out on the back porch.

The sound of a boat engine startled them. James looked down the hill to the dock and saw the boathouse doors were open. A fishing boat backed out. Before the boat could turn around, James was running down the hill with Glory right behind him. Brock spotted them through the kitchen window and raced out the back door.

They reached the dock as the fishing boat sped away leaving a white stream of wake splashing behind it. Brock grabbed his radio and called the van. "Get a chopper out here now and call the Coast Guard!" he ordered. "They're on Furman's fishing boat!"

Glory ran toward the boathouse. "He also has a speedboat!" she screamed over her shoulder. The men raced after her.

Evidently Will felt his speedboat was safely stored in the boathouse because the keys were sitting in the ignition. Glory started the engine, as the men jumped on board she backed out of the boathouse.

"Hang on!" she yelled over the roar of the boat engine. She turned the boat around and raced away from land. Gritting her teeth she willed the boat forward.

The speedboat lived up to its name as they roared toward open water. Will's fishing boat was barely visible on the horizon. Glory rammed the engine into high gear and the men grabbed hold of the bolted down deck chairs to keep from flying over the sides.

James watched in fascination as Glory raced toward the fishing boat. They were flying across the water; the prow of the boat high in the air, giant white water wakes streaming out behind them.

Will heard the speedboat engine's roar and watched as it began gaining on them. He began shooting at them while Parker pushed the fishing boat to its limit trying to escape.

Bullets flew by their heads and slapped into the water beside the speedboat. They were moving too fast for Will's aim to be accurate. As they got closer to the fishing boat, Brock made Glory slow down as he took aim to return fire.

The first shot from Brock's pistol missed Will, hitting the deck beside his leg. Will dropped to the deck and fired back. Brock fired again and hit the deck by Will's head causing him to scoot back toward the wheelhouse.

James planted his feet apart on the moving floor of the boat. Using both hands to steady his shot, he pointed his revolver toward Parker. The wheelhouse had no third wall and was open on the back. James held his breath and slowly pulled the trigger. The bullet hit Parker in the shoulder jerking him sideways. Parker lost hold of the steering wheel and the boat began turning in a wide circle. He lurched forward and grabbed the wheel to straighten their course, but their speed had dropped off and the other boat was gaining fast.

Blood ran down Parker's shoulder and suddenly he felt dizzy. He couldn't hold on to the wheel with one hand and put pressure on his wounded shoulder at the same time. He knew their flight was over. He began slowing the boat.

By now Glory had the speedboat running right beside the fishing boat. Brock lowered his gun, stepped up onto a chair and leapt onto the other deck beside Will's prostrate form.

Before Will could react Brock slammed a fist into his face. Stunned, Will dropped his weapon. Brock flung Will onto his back, pulled his arms behind him and slapped handcuffs on his wrists.

James jumped on to the fishing boat and walked toward Parker who was sitting on the floor holding his shoulder.

"Don't shoot," begged Parker, his face pale.

James holstered his gun and turned off the fishing boat's engine. It sputtered to a stop.

"Where's Michel?" asked James, leaning down and getting in Parker's face.

Parker nodded to a lumpy piece of tarp pushed up against the side of the boat.

James reached over and pulled up the tarp. Michel was unconscious with his hands and feet tied. A bloody rag was tied around one hand. "You were going to throw him overboard?" asked James aghast.

"Will was waiting for him to wake up to ask him some questions," said Parker.

"Then what?"

Parker shrugged which hurt his shoulder and he grimaced. "Then overboard."

James clenched his fists. He wanted to punch Parker but restrained himself.

The thrumming sound of a helicopter caused them to look overhead.

The SWAT chopper hovered a few yards behind them stirring up the water and blowing anything loose around on the boat. Brock waved them back and they retreated to a safer distance.

A Coast Guard cruiser ran up beside the fishing boat and an EMT jumped onto the deck with a satchel. He hurried over as James removed the tarp from the still form of Michel.

The EMT checked Michel's vital signs. He shook his head, "His blood pressure and pulse are too low." He lifted Michel's eyelids and shined a small penlight at them. The pupils were unequal. "He's got a concussion," he said, feeling the lump on the side of Michel's skull. "We need to get him to a hospital."

"What about me?" whined Parker. "I'm bleeding."

Brock walked up to him. "I'll take you to the hospital myself," he growled.

Parker flinched and slid back against the wall away from Brock.

After putting a neck brace on Michel, James and the EMT carefully carried him over to the Coast Guard vessel. They strapped him on a stretcher and the boat roared off.

"You take the speedboat back to the boathouse and park it," Brock hollered to Glory. "I'll drive this one back after I radio for an ambulance to meet me at the dock. The SWAT team can take care of William Furman," he said pushing at Will with the toe of his boot.

Will grunted and glared at Brock. If looks could kill, Brock would be full of bullets.

Brock grinned and waved at Glory. "By the way, good job, Officer Dayes."

Glory nodded and turned the speedboat back toward shore.

## Chapter 30

Back at William Furman's house the SWAT and CSI teams were tearing the place apart. The drug dog found traces of cocaine in cracks on the kitchen table and one of the team found the container of rat poison in the basement.

Brock and Glory stood outside on the front porch each in deep phone conversations with their respective bosses.

"Yes, Sir, we found the young man," said Glory. "He was alive. I don't know, he was unconscious but the Coast Guard is taking him to the hospital in Portland." She listened for a few minutes in silence. "Thank you, Sir. I'll let you know what we find in the house." She ended the call and slipped her phone in a back pocket.

Brock ended his call as a member of the SWAT team stepped onto the front porch. "You need to come see this," said the man. They stopped outside the door to put paper booties over their shoes and gloves on their hands. He led them upstairs to Will's bedroom.

The room smelled gamey with sweat and dirty clothes. They stepped over piles of dirty clothing and shoes when they entered. Dirty crumpled sheets covered the bed. What was visible of the carpet desperately needed vacuuming.

A German shepherd sat panting beside the open closet door. "Trudy's got a good nose," bragged the officer. "All I can smell is the stench in the room. She found this." He pointed inside the closet.

Brock stepped closer and saw the opened panel in the back of the closet. A CSI member was snapping photos of the hidden panel and its contents. When he finished they removed the items one-by-one as he took more photos.

A full bag of white powder, a partial bag of powder, a pistol, and a metal box were placed on the floor beside the unmade, rumpled bed. Brock opened the full bag. The CSI agent used a tool to remove a small sample of the white powder. Using a colorimetric test kit he determined the substance was cocaine.

"It's high quality cocaine," he told Brock.

Brock opened the metal box and whistled at the stacks of $100 bills. He looked at the officer. "Be sure and count and log in the amount. We wouldn't want any of it to go missing."

Over the next few minutes each item was catalogued, photographed and bagged as evidence.

Brock patted Trudy's head. "Good dog," he said smiling. "You too, Officer Vincent."

Glory followed Brock back downstairs past several CSI members. They stopped as they passed the door to the kitchen. Dirty dishes covered the counters.

" I don't know how they find anything in this mess," said Glory in disgust.

"Officer Hamilton," called a woman dressed in white disposable CSI garb. "We found a box of rat poison. It will be analyzed at the lab to see if it matches the chemical that killed those two drug addicts."

Brock nodded. "Thanks, Bonnie. We'll need all the evidence we can get against these two. The DEA's been watching them for a while. I'd love for us to be the ones to help put them away for good."

####

At the Portland medical center, Michel was admitted to the ICU, Intensive Care Unit. After several hours the doctors were able to stabilize his vital signs, but he was still unconscious. Dr. Curtis Clifford, a neurologist, worked with him all through the night.

It was five o'clock in the morning when Dr. Clifford went to find James in the waiting room to give him an update on Michel's condition.

"I'm Dr. Clifford," he said, introducing himself to James. "You're the patient's father?"

"His step-father. I'm James Ford."

The doctor nodded. "Michel has a severe concussion. It doesn't appear that we'll need to do surgery to relieve the pressure as it is beginning to come down on its own. His hand was cut and two fingers broken but we've stitched up his palm and set the fingers. I've started him on antibiotics and a medicine to help reduce the swelling inside his skull."

"So we won't really know if there's lasting damage to his brain until the swelling goes down and he regains consciousness?" asked James.

"That's correct. You can visit him for a few minutes, but otherwise nothing much will happen for hours," said Dr. Clifford. "Follow me."

He led James down a hallway, punched a code into the locked door that buzzed and opened into the ICU area. They walked past the nurses' station. Michel was lying on a bed in a room with glass walls. The curtains on the walls were partially closed. When they entered the small room James recognized the cardiac monitor that beeped in a steady rhythm.

Michel was receiving oxygen through a facemask, IV fluids dripped into a site on his arm. He was covered with a white sheet up to his chest but some of the cardiac leads could be seen above the sheets. A bag on the side of the bed held yellow urine. His face was pale and he had a huge purple bruise on his temple. James walked to the side of the bed, but was afraid to touch him for fear of interfering with the machines.

A pumping noise started up as the blood pressure cuff on Michel's arm filled. When it finished the machine read 118/52. The pulse oxygen reader on one finger said his oxygen saturation was 99%. Those readings looked pretty good to James. There was no chair for him to sit down, so he stood beside the bed and watched the rise and fall of Michel's chest as he breathed.

"Your Mom's pretty worried about you, Michel," said James. "You need to get well."

A nurse came in and hung a bag of antibiotics on the IV pole then attached its tubing to the port on the side of Michel's IV line. She set the IV pump to deliver the antibiotics.

"He's been stable for the last hour," she told James. "He seems like a fighter and that will help him recover."

James nodded. "He is a fighter."

"I'm afraid you'll have to leave now. He's only allowed visitors for ten minutes each hour," informed the nurse. "There's a vending machine in the ICU waiting room and free coffee, if you're planning to stay a while."

"Thanks. But I've been up all night. I think I'll check into a hotel and get some sleep," he said. He gave her his cell phone number in case the doctor needed to contact him.

"There's a Hampton Inn a few blocks south of here," she said. "They give a discount if you have a family member in the hospital. And they have a pretty good breakfast buffet."

James nodded. "I'll give it a try."

James left the hospital and walked the few blocks to the hotel. They were already serving breakfast. He checked in, ate some scrambled eggs and a waffle, and went to his room. He called Lacey to give her an update then collapsed on the bed and fell asleep.

## Chapter 31

Parker Thomas was sweating. His shoulder hurt where he'd been wounded and he had a pounding headache. They'd moved him from his cell to the interrogation room twenty minutes ago. He picked up the bottle of water they'd given him and took a drink. He rubbed at the bandage on his shoulder under the orange jumpsuit. He hated jail clothing, orange wasn't a color he ever wore and the heavy black shoes were uncomfortable.

The door opened and Officer Brock Hamilton entered with another officer. Brock sat down across the table from Parker while the second man stood against the wall behind Parker.

Brock opened a manila folder he placed on the table. Even sitting down, Brock was a foot taller than Parker. His dark brown eyes stared down at the prisoner. Brock cleared his throat. "I'll be recording this interview, Parker," he said turning on the recorder.

Parker just shrugged.

Brock gave the date and time for the recording. "Interview of Parker Thomas," he said.

After reading for a few minutes from the papers, Brock shook his head and looked over at Parker. "Looks like you're in wicked bad trouble," said Brock in his deep voice.

Parker was silent but his hands started shaking as Brock's eyes bored into him. Parker looked away. He knew there were others watching through the fake mirror on the wall.

"Drug smuggling, drug sales and distribution, kidnapping, murder, fleeing the police, obstruction of justice, tsk, tsk," said Brock. "You've been a bad boy. What would your mother think of you, Parker?"

Parker's face blanched. "My mom's dead," he mumbled, casting his eyes down.

Brock shook his head. "Still, she must be watching you."

Parker shivered at the thought. His mother would be so disappointed in him. "Wait a minute," he said looking up at Brock. "Did you say murder? I ain't killed no one!"

Brock looked back down at the papers. "It says here you killed Belinda Hillman and Tommy Vince."

"No way!" said Parker. "That was Will. He put rat poison in the dope. I didn't have nothing to do with that. He even took the bags to them himself. Not me." Parker's face had gone from pale to bright red, as he got upset. "I ain't no murderer."

"So it was William Furman who poisoned Belinda and Tommy?" asked Brock to make certain the names were being recorded.

Parker nodded. "Yeah. And he's the one who shot that other guy."

Brock looked up from the papers, puzzled. "What other guy?"

"The scuba diver who was spying on us," said Parker, not sure now that he should have said anything. "The guy who disappeared over by Damariscove Island."

Brock looked through his papers. "I'll be back in a minute." He turned off the recorder and left the room.

Officers Glory Dayes, Devon Adams and Brent West were watching the interview behind the one-way glass mirror on the wall of the interrogation room.

Glory met Brock in the hallway. "He's talking about Richard Prescott. He was a lobsterman who disappeared two years ago. We found his body the night they attacked us and kidnapped Michel," she explained. "We still need to go back out there and get his body out of an underwater cave on the island."

"Huh," said Brock. "I guess I never heard about that."

Brock went back in the interrogation room and sat down. He turned on the recorder. "The man you're talking about is Richard Prescott," he said.

"I guess so," said Parker. "I didn't know his name. All I know is Will sold the guy's boat to some French man in Canada."

"You be willing to testify to all this in court?"

Parker looked scared. "Against Will?"

"If you say he murdered these people, not you, then you have to testify to that," warned Brock. "You brave enough to do that, Parker?"

Parker nodded and stuck out his chin. "Well, it's true, so I guess so."

"Now Parker, the judge will go easier on you if you tell us who William's supplier is."

Parker's face went stark white at the thought. "Those guys from New York are scary. I don't know if I should rat on them."

Brock glared at him. "Suit yourself, but if they're in prison, they won't be able to hurt you. If they learn about your and Will's arrest, they might be pretty pissed off," noted Brock. "And I'm sure they'll hear about it."

Parker's body began shaking.

"Telling me who they are might be the only way for you to stay safe," warned Brock.

Glory, Devon and Brent held their breath as they collectively leaned closer to the window. "Do you think he'll give up the names?" wondered Devon.

"If he gives up the suppliers that would be a major win," observed Brent. The others nodded and continued watching.

Parker was shaking so hard his chair rattled against the floor.

"Come on, Parker. Guys like those suppliers in New York can reach you even in prison if they're out on the street," encouraged Brock. "You don't want to spend the rest of your pitiful days looking over your shoulder, do you?"

Parker looked up at Brock. "If they go to prison will it be down in New York?"

"They'll go to a federal prison. It won't be anywhere near Maine," promised Brock.

Parker took a deep breath. "The head guy is Earl Childs," he said.

Brock smiled. "We've heard of him."

"His goon is a really mean looking guy with lots of tattoos. He's good at hurting people Earl doesn't like. I only remember his first name is Sonny."

"We know about him, too. He's Sonny Weather. You're right about him being mean," said Brock. "You've been really helpful, Parker." Brock stood up. "We'll have some papers for you to sign in a little bit. So you need anything?"

Parker nodded. "My shoulder hurts like hell and I have a headache."

"I'll make sure you get something for that," promised Brock. "This interview ended at ten thirty-for." Brock turned off the recorder.

The officers watching the interview looked at each other and smiled.

Glory gloated, "I knew Parker was the weak link."

"Good thing, 'cause William isn't saying anything," said Devon. "I don't think he'll ever admit a thing."

"Now maybe we can get some of the drugs off our streets," she observed.

"Don't get your hopes up," warned Bren, shaking his head. "When there's a vacuum seems like someone moves in to fill it pretty fast."

Glory sighed. "I think you're right about that. It's a losing battle."

Devon patted her shoulder. "This will help for a while. We just do the best we can."

## Chapter 32

James picked up Lacey at the Portland Jetport at three o'clock. She was tired and frazzled, but wanted to go straight to the hospital to see Michel. James parked the car and led her to the ICU floor. When they pushed the buzzer by the door a nurse at the desk let them in.

"We're getting him ready to be moved to a Medical/Surgical room," the nurse told them as they approached the desk for an update on Michel's condition.

"So he's that much better?" asked Lacey.

"See for yourself," said the nurse pointing to Michel's room.

When they walked into the room, they were surprised to see Michel sitting up in bed drinking apple juice. He looked up and grinned at them. "Hi, Mom."

"I can't believe you're awake," said James. "This morning you were practically comatose." He stepped up to the bed and patted Michel's shoulder.

"Mom, I'm sorry you had to come all the way back up here," apologized Michel. "I'm going to be fine according to the doctor."

Tears ran down Lacey's cheeks as she leaned over to hug him. "You couldn't have kept me away after what happened," she said, wiping at the tears. "I would have wanted to see for myself that you were all right."

"I have a headache and I'm hungry, but otherwise fine," he promised. "They've got me on a clear liquid diet. No food until tomorrow."

"Gosh, I don't know how you'll make it that long," laughed Lacey.

"Is Lily with grandma?" asked Michel.

Lacey nodded. "We'll have to Skype with her so they can see how well you're doing."

James shook his head. "I can't believe how much better you look from this morning. It's a complete change."

"What happened to your hand?" asked Lacey lightly touching his bandaged hand.

Michel grimaced. "I was using a piece of broken glass to cut the rope they tied around my wrists. They caught me before I finished. One of them stomped on my hand," he explained. "The cut wasn't deep but he broke two fingers."

Lacey's eyes widened and her face turned red. "I'd like to stomp on his face!" she muttered. "I'm glad the police caught both those men."

James laughed. "Right now that's all that's keeping them safe from your mother," he said grinning. "Lacey would give them a thrashing."

The curtains were pushed aside by a tall man in scrubs. "Doc said I can move you to your new room," said the burly man from the hospital transportation department.

While Michel was being moved out of ICU to another room, the doctor took his parents into a small consultation room.

"He's made a quick recovery," said Dr. Clifford. "I'm amazed myself at the numbers I've seen. The pressure inside his skull is normal and the CT scan showed no internal bleeding. He'll be fine in a few days."

"When will he be allowed to fly back home to Arkansas?" asked Lacey.

"I'll need to watch him for a few days," said Clifford. "If he doesn't develop any symptoms of post-concussion syndrome he should be able to go on an airplane by the end of the week. Flying will probably cause a headache but nothing permanent. It's the rushing around, noise and bright lights in the airport that can cause discomfort. If you have a wheelchair waiting for him that would help."

"Thank you for taking such good care of him," said Lacey.

Dr. Clifford smiled. "He did this on his own. He recovered faster than I expected."

When Michel was settled in his new room they Skyped with Amanda and Lily. Lily started crying when she saw the purple bruise on Michel's temple.

"I'd like to slug that mean man," she said between sniffles.

James laughed. "You're just like your mom. Two tough girls."

By the time they finished talking, Michel had made enough jokes to get Lily laughing.

"Michel, this will probably ruin your plans for starting college this fall," lamented Lacey.

"It'll be alright," he comforted. "I'll sign up for a few online classes. But I'll need someone to help with my keyboarding until these fingers heal."

"I don't think that will be a problem. Grandma and I can manage as long as you tell us what to type. I won't do your homework for you," she warned.

He laughed. "I didn't think you would. You never did it while I was in school. Not even the science projects." He leaned back on his pillow and grimaced.

"I think you've had enough excitement for a while," said Lacey patting his arm. "We should let you rest."

The nurse gave Michel something for pain. After he fell asleep James talked Lacey into going for dinner then a rest back at his hotel room. "We can come visit later," he promised.

####

The CSI team for the Rockland area instructed Glory and Brent West on what they would need to do when they went to collect Richard Prescott's body.

No one on the CSI team was adept at scuba diving and that put the responsibility on the 'Dive and Rescue' team members.

"Just take a ton of photos," instructed the lead CSI team member, a small black woman in her forties. Penny Langley wanted desperately to go see for herself and collect evidence but the idea of diving and crawling into a dark cave sent shivers down her spine. "You can't take too many pictures."

They loaded the camera and the evidence containers into a waterproof duffle bag along with a body bag. Glory was a little nervous about having Brent along as he was even bigger than Winston and she didn't know if he would fit through the cave's narrow opening and tunnel.

Winston agreed to take them out to the island on his boat and he insisted on diving with them. Glory got permission for him to accompany them because he had assisted the dive team in the past. It didn't hurt that he would provide free use of his boat.

They left Rockport Harbor at the break of dawn and reached Damariscove Island by ten thirty. Luckily it was a bright sunny day with calm winds. By the time they donned their dry-suits and tanks it was high tide with the calmest water.

"Winston stand behind Brent against his back so I can see how much bigger he is than you," instructed Glory.

"Beside topping me by six inches?" laughed Winston.

The two men stood back to back while she walked around them.

"Brent's shoulders are about four inches wider than yours," she noted. "It will be close but I think he can get through the tunnel."

"How big is the cave?" asked Brent. "Will we all fit inside?"

"Oh, it's huge. No problem once we're inside," assured Glory.

Officer Devon Adams would stay on board the boat in case there were any problems he would be able to radio for help. A Coast Guard vessel was docked nearby at Boothbay Harbor.

Winston was the first one in the water followed by Glory then Brent who carried the duffle bag. It took ten minutes to find the cave. They all turned on their underwater flashlights and took stock of the cave opening.

It was decided that Brent would bring up the rear in case he had trouble moving forward. That way if he had to back out, the others wouldn't be in his way. Glory was the smallest and she would tow the duffle bag. After they worked all that out, Winston dove into the cave opening.

The distance to the cave seemed shorter now that they were familiar with what they would find as they swam. Glory had a little trouble pulling the duffle behind her, but Brent pushed at it whenever it got stuck in a narrow spot and that helped.

Brent watched Glory's swim fins and the duffle in front of him. It was a little unnerving not being able to see anything else in front. In some spots the tunnel walls were barely two inches wider than his shoulders and he had to twist sideways to get through. Good thing I'm not claustrophobic, he thought as he squeezed through a particularly tight area.

At the upward turn, Brent managed to bend enough to get through. They all removed their facemasks once they reached the edge of the sandy shore inside the cave. They left their tanks way off to one side out of the way.

Glory unpacked the camera while the men set their flashlights on high beam and flooded the body with light. They stayed back out of her way while she took photos from every angle.

"What should we gather for evidence," asked Winston, holding up the evidence bags. His voice echoed eerily around the cave.

"Anything that belonged to him or that looks out of place, I guess," said Brent. "Like his flashlight." He pointed to the rusty flashlight lying next to the body.

Winston put on gloves and retrieved the flashlight, bagged it and Brent labeled the bag. They gathered Richard's discarded facemask.

"So this is your father?" asked Brent.

"Yeah. Pretty strange to finally find him like this."

"I can only imagine," said Brent.

"Should we bring out his tank?" asked Winston.

"Yes, we'll need to try to get that, too. It might take two trips to get everything," said Brent. He walked closer to study the body.

Hermit crabs had scavenged Richard's flesh that wasn't covered by his dry-suit and Brent tried not to get too freaked out by the bare skull.

"This is what killed him," said Glory. She leaned closer and a close-up photo of the hole in the dry-suit's thigh area. "He was shot and managed to swim in here but he had no way to stop the bleeding."

"He was probably pretty weak by the time he made it through the tunnel," observed Brent. "He managed to get his mask off but not much else."

"Except this," said Winston. He pointed to the seashell scratches on the wall of the cave near Richard's head.

"Oh, yeah," said Brent, leaning down to read the writing.

*Tell wife + son love them. Richard*

Glory took several photos of the writing. Brent bagged the broken piece of white shell by Richard's bony fingers.

The men rolled Richard's body over and Glory took more photos of his back.

"Looks like the bullet didn't come out the back of his suit," she observed. "The coroner can find that when he does the autopsy. We can compare it to William Furman's weapons."

After forty minutes they figured they had everything they needed. Glory helped Brent slide the body into the body bag and zipped it up.

"I think we can get everything in one trip," said Brent after attaching Richard's empty air tank beside Winston's tank on his back.

Winston swam with the evidence duffle while Glory and Brent maneuvered the body bag.

They'd exited the cave opening and were headed to the surface when a dark shadow blocked the sunlight shining through the water above them.

Winston pointed up. A huge white shark swam ten feet over their heads. They dropped to the ocean bottom and huddled down in the long kelp. The shark swam in circles for a few minutes then passed by overhead.

As the shark moved out of sight, they slowly kicked their way to the surface dragging the duffle and body bag. When they broke surface near the boat, Devon hurried over to help them up the boat ladder. Winston handed Devon the evidence bag then climbed on board.

Glory reached the ladder but couldn't lift her end of the body bag. Devon leaned over to help her lift while Brent pushed from his end.

They almost had the bag on the deck when Devon slipped and plunged head first into the water. He came up sputtering as Brent shoved his end of the body bag onto the deck.

Before he could swim back to the ladder Devon felt something huge bump into his leg.

The shark swam past Devon. It was circling back when Devon shouted for help. Brent saw what was happening and hurriedly swam to Devon's side.

The shark swam straight for Devon with its mouth open. When Brent pushed Devon toward the boat, he frantically swam to the ladder. Winston leaned over and pulled Devon onboard.

Brent waited for the shark to get within striking distance. As the big white nose edged toward him, he braced himself. Doubling his fists together he slammed them into the shark's face. The shark closed its mouth and Brent punched again, this time hitting it in the eye.

The shark dove beneath Brent deciding whatever this strange creature was it didn't want to eat it. As the shark descended, Brent swam with all his might toward the boat.

Winston reached down and grabbed Brent's tank to help him climb up the ladder.

Brent yanked off his facemask and started laughing.

The others looked at him in shock. They were still trying to figure out how he hadn't been bitten.

"That's the first time I ever had a fist fight with a shark," barked Brent gasping for breath. "I need a beer." He was grinning from ear to ear, his brown eyes sparkling, water dripping off his dark face and hair.

Glory looked at Winston and they both burst out laughing.

In a most uncharacteristic move, Devon reached up and hugged Brent. "You saved my life, man. I can't begin to pay you back."

Still laughing, Brent winked at Glory. "I guess you'll be the one buying coffee for the next few months," he said.

"You got it, man." Devon stepped back and grinned.

## Chapter 33
## New York

Earl Childs was sitting on his private balcony in his six million dollar condo on John Street with a view of the Brooklyn Bridge enjoying the last of the sunshine before sunset. Earl wore a smoking jacket he'd purchased at an auction that once belonged to Howard Hughes. He fancied himself on par with the famous millionaire.

For the umpteenth time he was laughing about the look on William Furman's face when he left the poker game in Miami after losing $15,000.

Sonny Weather had listened to his boss rehash the story so many times he was sick of it. He rolled his eyes and took a sip of his beer. "Yeah, he looked sick, all right."

"That country hick thought he was so slick," laughed Earl.

"Guess youse showed him, huh, Boss," said Sonny, also for the umpteenth time.

"Sure did." Earl swallowed the last of the expensive bourbon in his glass and leaned back with a sigh. "Life's great, isn't it? Wonder when he'll want another shipment," he mused.

Sonny shrugged. He didn't like traveling all the way to backwoods Maine to deliver drugs. He preferred big cities where they could hide in the crowds.

Earl got off his lounge chair and went to pour himself another drink. He looked around his luxurious condo and smiled to himself. Black leather couches and chairs, glass top tables, expensive Oriental rugs and original paintings filled the place. He was proud of himself. He was a self-made man, an important one at that. He ruled the Brooklyn cocaine trade and was getting ready to expand his business. He had plans to destroy the gang who held Manhattan.

Sonny followed Earl into the living room and watched him pour another bourbon over fresh ice in the crystal tumbler. "I should be going, Boss," he said.

"Aw, hang around for a little longer," urged Earl. "We can check out the new porno station. Maybe we can find another movie with that blond bombshell."

Sonny reluctantly agreed. But he really wanted to go home and go to bed, it was after seven o'clock and he was tired of listening to Earl's ramblings.

Neither one of the men were aware of the action down on the street fourteen floors below the condo apartment. A New York City SWAT team van pulled up behind the DEA SUV parked on the street. Local police officers had cordoned off John Street and vacated the premises on the floors above and below Earl's condo. DEA agents using a scrambling device made it impossible for Earl to receive a phone call of warning. An ambulance was parked nearby.

The DEA's investigation of Earl Childs had been building for eleven months and the witness statement from Parker Thomas gave them the last piece of evidence they needed. It had been hard to build a case against Earl in New York. None of the addicts would talk for fear of losing their supply and the pushers were all terrified of Sonny.

The two teams entered the building then split up. One prearranged group took the elevator and the second one took the stairs. Local police officers were left guarding the second elevator and front door. They knew from their surveillance that both Earl and Sonny were upstairs.

Although he was in good physical shape, Brock Hamilton was glad to be in an elevator. He didn't want to be out of breath from climbing fourteen flights of stairs when he confronted the two men. Brock and his team waited outside Earl's front door until the second team exited the stairwell.

The biggest man Brock had ever met walked up to him with a grin. Sylvester Connor stood six foot seven and weighed three hundred pounds of solid muscle. Wearing full riot gear he was a formidable presence. Brock hoped the sight of him would subdue even Sonny.

Brock nodded and Sylvester kicked in Earl's front door.

As soon as the door crashed open, Brock yelled into the foyer. "Police! Freeze and put your hands up!"

Earl and Sonny, engrossed in a particularly vivid porn scene, were taken totally by surprise. Earl looked up when he heard the door crash open and scrambled for the gun he kept in the small table beside the couch.

Sonny stared at the men rushing toward him. His mouth hung open and his brain refused to believe what just happened. Before he could decide what to do, a man the size of a giant grabbed him by the shoulders and threw him to the floor. With his knee on Sonny's back, Sylvester pulled Sonny's hands behind him and handcuffed them together.

Sylvester yanked the stunned Sonny to his feet and marched him to the foyer where he patted him down. He removed a pistol and switchblade knife and handed them to another officer. Sonny was too stunned to protest. He found it hard to believe what had just happened.

Earl in the meantime retrieved his revolver. He backed toward the balcony door pointing the gun at the officers. "I'm not going with you," he said calmly.

"Put the gun down, Earl," said Brock. "You're outnumbered."

That was obvious to Earl as he looked at the six men standing in his living room pointing assault rifles at him. He took another step backwards.

Brock stepped forward with his hands outstretched, his revolver still holstered. "Come on, Earl. Nobody needs to get hurt today."

Earl shook his head. He didn't like this guy with the strange accent. Sounded like he was from Australia or New Zealand. Instead Earl kept slowly backing toward the balcony. When he reached the door he used his left hand to open it outward. He stepped through onto the tile floor outside. It was dark now. Only the lights of the Manhattan skyline lit the area behind him.

"What are you doing. Earl?" asked Brock. "There's no where to go out there." He led the officers slowly toward the open door.

Earl kept backing away past the chairs until he reached the metal railing surrounding the outside edge of the balcony. Earl glanced down while keeping his gun pointed at Brock.

Brock knew what Earl planned, but he had no intention of letting this evil man get off so easily. Earl needed to stand trial and spend the rest of his life in prison.

"Don't do it, Earl," said Brock. "Let's talk about this."

"I'm not going to prison," said Earl shaking his head and glancing at the steep drop to the street below. Red and blue lights flashed brightly in the darkness.

While earl was looking down, Brock upholstered his revolver. Before he could jump, Brock shot Earl in the knee.

Earl screamed and fell to the floor as blood drenched Earl's pant leg. He tried to pull himself up by grabbing the railing. He was halfway over the rail when Brock tackled him to the floor. He twisted Earl onto his stomach and handcuffed him.

"Nice jacket, Earl," quipped Brock. "Hope the blood washes out."

Earl was actually crying big crocodile tears when two SWAT team members pulled him to his feet and practically carried him inside. They plopped him down on the couch.

"This is police brutality," he shouted. "My knee's ruined!"

An EMT bandaged Earl's knee while agents began searching the condo.

Earl glared at Brock. "You won't find anything here," he sneered. "And nobody in New York with testify."

"Really?" said Brock. "Guess we'll just have to rely on the dealers in Maine."

Earl's eyes widened and he showed the first signs of fear.

As soon as his knee was bandaged two EMT's half carried Earl down to the ambulance and along with an armed police officer he was taken to the nearest hospital.

After scouring the condo for hours, Brock had to admit that there were no drugs here. One of the officers came up to him and handed him a key. "I found this in his desk," he said. "Do you think it's for a storage place?"

Brock examined the key. "Yes, I think it is and I know just where to look."

"How do you know that?"

"See this little red symbol?" He pointed to a squiggle on the key. "I've seen it before."

That afternoon the agents swarmed to the storage facility with a full CSI team. The man in the office showed them the rental agreement for the storage room with Earl's signature.

Brock showed him a photo of Earl.

The man nodded. "That's the guy who rented unit number 1143."

"Thanks for your help," said Brock. "I'll need a copy of that agreement."

DEA agents found bags of cocaine, boxes of pills and a pile of money tucked in a metal box. A small briefcase held more cash and two different passports.

Brock was the one who found the small black notebook that held the names and phone numbers of all of his dealers. He held up the book, grinning. "The boys in charge will be happy to see this," he said. "I'm afraid Earl's going away for a long time."

All in all, Brock was pleased with the results.

## Chapter 34
## Maine

Michel was released from the hospital with orders to rest and not to fly home for one week. He needed to return for a final check-up with the doctor to be approved to get on an airplane. The three of them drove north in the rental car to Thomaston to stay with Annette and Winston. They arrived before lunch and as usual Annette had food waiting for them.

Michel made short work of three ham and cheese sandwiches with chips and sliced apples. After his third glass of milk Winston teased him.

"Where do you put all that food?" asked Winston. "Even I can't eat that much."

Michel finished off the milk and grinned. "I was starved in the hospital. Clear liquids, then full liquids, then a soft diet. Ugh. My last day there I was finally approved for solid food and what did they send me? An indeterminate meat patty, mashed potatoes, and mushy carrots."

"You did eat all of it," pointed out Lacey.

"I had to or I would have fainted from starvation," he complained.

Annette was laughing so hard she had trouble speaking. "I guess that means you still have room for a slice of chocolate cake?"

A big grin split Michel's face. "Can I have two pieces?"

While Michel sat alone at the table finishing his meal, the others went into the living room to talk.

Winston looked at James. "Glory and I want to go back down to the cave," he said. "But it would be safer if we had someone with us. Would you and Lacey be willing to go out again?"

"Sure we would," said Lacey.

"What do you hope to find?" asked James.

Winston shrugged. "I don't know. We covered every inch of the front of cave when we removed dad's body. But no one has gone to the back of it. You remember how big it was. Maybe there's still something there. "

James nodded. " I remember our lights didn't even reach the back wall."

"That's why I have to go back. My father thought there was something in that cave. I want to see if he was right." Winston picked up his father's notebook and papers from the coffee table. "He described all his research in this little book." He handed it to James.

Lacey scooted over next to James on the sofa and they looked through the notebook together. After a few minutes Lacey asked, "When did you want to go out?"

"Well, Glory has tomorrow off," Winston explained. "After that she doesn't have another free day until next week. You'll be gone by then."

"Hopefully," said Lacey. "But only if they release Michel to fly home." She looked at James. "I'm happy to go tomorrow and stay on the boat while you three dive."

"Sounds like a plan," agreed James. "I'll go rent a dry-suit this afternoon."

Michel wandered in from the kitchen and they told him their plans.

"I wish I could dive," he said then looked at his mother. "I know I can't. Besides the fact that my hand is still bandaged, I don't think the doctor would approve of the extra pressure on my head under that much water."

"I'm sorry, Michel," said Lacey.

He sighed. "I think I need to go take a nap. This morning wore me out."

As he headed for the stairs, Winston jumped up and followed him. "I'm taking the top bunk while you're here," he informed Michel. "Can't have you falling off the top bunk, you'd end up with permanent brain damage."

Michel punched him in the arm then said, "Thanks."

####

The three of them left early the next morning to catch high tide when they reached the Damariscove Island. Now that September was here, the weather would be decidedly chilly out on the water. Lacey wore one of Annette's sweatshirts over her own shirt. She also had on long pants. It was no longer weather for summer clothing.

Glory hugged Lacey when they met at the Rockport dock. "I'm glad Michel's OK", she whispered. "We were all worried."

"He's almost fully recovered," said Lacey smiling.

Winston piloted the boat out of the harbor and they all settled down for the long ride.

Damariscove Island looked forlorn with no tourists or boats at the dock. Only a few seagull calls broke the stillness. The sun was shining but didn't warm the air and the cool breeze picked up after they anchored Winston's boat off the Atlantic side of the island.

"It's always cooler on the eastern coast of the islands," said Winston.

"I'm glad you warned me before we left," said Lacey. "Your mom's sweatshirt helps."

Winston reminded Lacey how to use the radio in case they had a problem.

They spent ten minutes getting into the dry-suits and putting on their tanks. Winston scanned the water for any sign of sharks. He didn't want a repeat of last time.

"The water looks pretty clear," he observed looking into the dark blue water. "We haven't had any big storms yet to stir up the bottom. It sometimes gets bad later in the year."

James dropped into the water first, followed by Glory then Winston. They waved to Lacey and disappeared.

There seemed to be a lot more fish in the area around the rocky island reef than the last time they dived. Winston hoped that was because the sharks left the area. A school of alewives swam past him, some of them rubbing his shoulder with their small silvery bodies. There was a large lobster peeking out between two rocks. The reef was alive with fish and he spotted sand eels and sea snails on the rocks as well as a starfish.

Winston found the cave opening. The seaweed and kelp were still thick but he could see areas where it had been flattened when they came to remove his father's remains. He pushed through the waving dark green strands of kelp and waited at the opening for the others.

They switched on their flashlights and Winston led the way inside. It seemed familiar now that he'd been here a few times. When his head broke the water surface he ran his light around the inside shore. There were only a few hermit crabs on the sand that scattered when he climbed out of the water and removed his mask.

They left their swim fins and tanks in a pile on the rocks.

Turning their flashlights to high beam they walked past the spot where they'd found Richard's body. It took several minutes and another twenty feet before their lights could reach the back wall. They scrambled around the stalagmites and sharp rocks to protect their bare feet.

They moved forward sweeping their lights back and forth from the floor to the ceiling and back down. There appeared to be some disturbance in the far right hand corner of the cave. Stalagmites were broken off and pushed to one side.

"Someone's been here before us," commented James.

As they moved toward the area Glory pointed to one side. "For heavens sake, there's a shovel!" Sure enough a rusted short-handled shovel like campers used leaned against the cave wall. "Looks like it's been here a long time."

They walked over to a corner of the cave. Several broken pieces of wood lay on the rocky floor. Their lights picked up the outline of a broken wooden box. It was two feet long and one foot wide. Parts of the lid lay on the ground with an old rusted lock still in place. The top had been smashed open.

Winston knelt down beside the box. "I guess someone couldn't get the lock open so they smashed the lid." He waved them over and their combined lights shone inside the empty box.

"Oh darn," said Glory. "They took whatever was inside."

They all stared at the wooden bottom of the box.

"But this means my father was right," observed Winston. "There was something here at one time. I wonder how old this box is."

When James shined his light to the broken top of the box faint painted letters appeared. They combined their lights and were barely able to read *W C Skinners, London.*

"Holy Crap!" exclaimed Winston. "Dad's notebook listed historical facts about the pirate Dixce Bull. He worked for a company in London called the *Worshipful Company of Skinners.* This box must have been made in the early 1600's!"

"That pirate wouldn't have hidden the box in a cave if it didn't have something important in it," sighed Glory.

"Wish I knew what he hid," complained Winston.

James was silent for a few seconds then nudged Winston's arm. "Maybe that will tell you." The light from James' flashlight pointed inside to the corner of the box where a small glint of gold shone on the bottom edge.

Glory added her light and Winston leaned down to get a closer look.

Jammed upright between the bottom of the box and a crack in the wooden side was a piece of metal. Using his fingernails Winston scraped at the metal. After a few minutes the object popped out of the crack and Winston picked it up.

He held the object out on the palm of his hand. It was a gold *SOVEREIGN*.

"Holy Smoke," said Glory. "That box must have been full of those coins and someone missed this one. What do you think its worth?"

The coin had the imprint of a queen facing to her left with a crown on her head.

"We can take it to a coin shop and ask someone," said Winston grinning.

After searching the ground and lifting the remains of the box, they determined there was nothing else left to find.

"I can't believe your father figured this out," said Glory.

They donned their equipment and left the cave. They swam to the surface and headed back to the boat.

They all started talking at once when they climbed aboard and removed their facemasks.

"Hold it," Lacey said. "One at a time."

"My dad was right!" Winston opened his palm and showed her the coin. "This was all that was left of the Dread Pirate Dixce Bull's treasure."

## Chapter 35

"Hi, Mom, where's Michel?" asked Lily as soon as the Skype phone call was answered.

"Well, hi to you, too," said James.

"Sorry, Daddy," apologized Lily.

James laughed. "It's OK. I know you're worried about Michel."

"I'm right here, Lily," said Michel moving into her view on the little camera. He turned his head to show her his bruised temple. "See, the bruise is almost gone now and I'm not having any headaches. So I'm doing fine."

Lily's face lit up and her blue eyes sparkled. "Thank goodness! Does that mean you can fly home now?"

"I won't know for sure until I see the neurologist on Friday," he said.

Lily sighed. "OK. But you look much better."

Lacey took over the call and began asking Lily questions about school and her friends. When she was satisfied with the answers she said, "Winston wants to show you something."

Lily looked puzzled. "Winston does?"

"Yup, I do," said Winston. "Remember when we went to Damariscove Island on my boat for a picnic?"

"Sure I do. That was so fun."

"And how you heard Michel and me talking about pirate treasure?" Winston grinned as he held up the gold sovereign. "Guess what we found in the underwater cave."

Lily's mouth fell open. "Wow, real pirate treasure. Wait 'til I tell the kids at school."

"I'll send you a picture to show your friends. But we only found one coin. Someone else found the treasure box and this was the only one they missed," he explained.

"But it's still pirate treasure."

Winston nodded. "It certainly is. We don't know how much it's worth yet. I have to show it to a coin expert to find out."

"That's really neat."

Lacey ended the call after talking to her mother.

"Are you going to see the coin expert in Camden today?" Michel asked Winston.

Winston nodded. "I have an appointment at one o'clock. You want to come?"

"I sure do. I couldn't dive with you, but at least I can hear what he says."

####

Winston parked his truck in front of the main library in Camden a few minutes before one. He carried the coin in a small plastic envelope to protect it from any more fingerprints that could tarnish it. Both men were dressed up a little each wearing slacks and button-up shirts instead of shorts. Winston had his red hair pulled back into a ponytail.

When they got inside the library the woman at the front desk pointed to an office in the back. She wore her brown hair in a chignon and wore wire frame glasses. She looked like a stereotypical librarian.

"Mr. Manning is our antique coin expert," she told them. "May I see the coin?"

Winston held up the clear bag and the gold coin shone in the overhead lights.

"Oh, it's lovely. Mr. Manning will be so excited."

Albert Manning was a sixty-four year old with a PHD in Library Science, but his hobby was studying old coins. He was short and rotund with a full gray mustache and head of hair. He wore his standard brown slacks, buttoned-down collar shirt and a bow tie. He stood up in excitement as Winston knocked on his office door.

"Come in, come in. I can't wait to see this fabulous coin. Albert Manning at your service," he said smiling.

"Winston Prescott and this is my cousin Michel Woods."

"Pleased to met you both," said Manning.

Winston handed him the bag with the coin.

Manning sat down at his large wooden desk. The padded desk chair squeaked as he rolled it closer to the desktop. He reached into a drawer and pulled out a pair of white cotton gloves and put them on. Only then did he open the envelope and touch the coin.

He peered at it then turned on a desk lamp and held it under the beam. He turned it over and studied the back. After reverently placing the coin on a piece of clean white paper, he pulled a magnifying glass out of a drawer and studied the front of the coin. All this time he had remained silent and Winston held his breath.

Finally Mr. Manning looked up as if he noticed for the first time that his visitors were still standing. "Oh dear. Please be seated," he said.

The men pulled two straight-backed wooden chairs closer to the desk and sat down.

Manning picked up a book on his desk and began flipping through the pages. He found the spot he was looking for and propped the book open. He scanned the short article then sat back in his chair and sighed. He smiled and looked at Winston.

"What you have found in a very rare *Elizabeth 1 Half Pound* gold coin," said Manning. "Wherever did you find this?"

Winston explained about his father's obsession with Dixce Bull and how he figured out there was a possibility that treasure was somewhere on Damariscove Island. "We found the underwater cave," said Winston excitedly. "And a broken wooden treasure box, but this was the only coin left inside. Someone had been there before us."

"Whoever it was must have found them many years ago otherwise such a find would be certain to make the news," said Manning.

"That's what we figured."

"Well," said Manning. "You're father certainly figured it out, didn't he? I'd like to meet him and ask about his research."

Winston frowned. "I'm afraid that's not possible. My father was murdered. We found his body in the cave."

Manning's eyes widened and his mouth dropped open. "My goodness. I'm so sorry."

"I do have his notebook and papers if you would like to review them."

"Oh yes. That would be delightful," said Manning. "Now let me tell you about this coin."

Manning launched into a detailed history of the coin.

"In 1558 when Queen Elizabeth-the-first began her reign she recalled all the base silver coins which were still in circulation. She replaced them with coins of a high silver content. The coins were milled from 1562 to 1571. *Milled* is the term used because the first machines were powered by water mills that allowed the strips of metal blanks to be cut into a consistent thickness for the coins. In gold, the milled coinage consisted of only a limited number of half-pounds with a value of ten shillings. They also struck coins called crowns worth five shillings and rare half-crowns worth two shillings and sixpence. They were all well-struck and circular in shape," he explained. "What you have here is extremely rare as these coins were only minted from 1550 to 1556. This is amazing."

Winston nodded. "That means the coins were available to Dixce Bull in the early 1600's. My Dad was right."

"That is the right time period." Manning beckoned for them to look closer at the coin with his magnifying glass.

"This coin is in mint condition. You can see the image of the crowned bust of Queen Elizabeth wearing a ruff and embroidered dress." He turned the coin over with his gloved fingers. "On the back is a shield quartered with the arms of France and England. The translation of the letters means *the shield of faith shall protect her*."

Michel nodded. "I can see it plainly. It's not worn or scratched at all."

Manning smiled. "You're right."

Winston looked up. "About how much is it worth?"

"I'd have to look it up," said Manning. "I have no idea off the top of my head. Let me do some research and I'll get back to you. You need to keep this protected from being touched at all. I have a coin case you can keep it in." He opened a bottom drawer and placed the coin in a small plastic case, which snapped shut. "You should lock this up somewhere safe."

Manning handed the coin to Winston. "Once word gets out people will be swarming Damariscove Island looking for treasure," he warned.

"I never thought of that," said Winston frowning.

"Treasure hunters would ruin that lovely place," said Manning.

"We'll keep it quiet," promised Winston thinking that he needed to warn Glory not to tell anyone about the coin. "Thank you for all your help." He wrote his phone number on a piece of paper and handed it back to Manning.

"I'll get back to you soon," said Manning.

When they got home Winston called Glory. He told her everything they'd learned about the coin. "Have you mentioned this to anyone?" he asked.

"Not a soul," she said. "I figured it was your story to tell."

"Well, I probably shouldn't tell anyone," he said then explained about treasures hunters.

"You're right. My lips are sealed," she promised.

####

The next morning Winston was out on his lobster boat when he got the call from Mr. Manning. "Morning, sir. I'm anxious to hear what you found out."

"According to the latest information I could find, your coin is worth between $16,000 and $18,000. There hasn't been one on the market for almost fifteen years and that was purchased by a museum in England for $17,600," said Manning. "I did some checking to see if there was any word on someone else finding the balance of the coins. Back in 1875 thirty-five of those coins turned up in England. It's possible those were from that box you found."

Winston was speechless for a few seconds. "Wow, one coin is worth that much?"

"Maybe a little more. It would depend on if you sold it or auctioned it off. Imagine what a box full of them would be worth on today's market. It boggles the mind."

"But if I auction it, people will find out it came from the coast of Maine," worried Winston.

"Not if you went through an auction house in England and requested they not give out that information," said Manning.

"OK."

"Another thing. I looked up the laws in Maine for governing ownership of lost treasure," said Manning.

"Will the state take the coin from me?" asked Winston.

"No. If a find is considered lost by current dates, it has to be turned over to the police to see if anyone else can claim it," said Manning. "But if you have a bonafide treasure, most states including Maine, pretty much say 'finders keepers', so you're in luck. You'd have to have found it while not trespassing and I don't believe an undiscovered underwater cave belongs to the owner of Damariscove Island."

Winston grinned. "So it's legally mine."

"Yes, it certainly is. If you decide to sell or auction it, let me know," offered Manning. "I can point you in the direction of a buyer or an auction house."

"Thank you so much. I appreciate your help."

"Don't mention it, literally. Can't have someone questioning me where it came from," he laughed. "Besides, just getting to see an actual *Elizabeth 1 Half Pound* sovereign was fantastic."

After he hung up, Winston danced around the boat deck for a few minutes. He looked up at the sky and yelled, "Thanks, Dad!"

## Chapter 36

Michel was given doctor's approval to fly home to Arkansas when they took him back to Portland for his check-up. James made flight reservations for early Sunday morning, which meant they needed to stay at a hotel in Portland the night before to check in at the airport on time. They only had one full day left to spend with Annette and Winston.

Michel chose to go out with Winston to check his lobster traps and they left the house at five o'clock in the morning. They wanted to have the evening off to attend a BBQ party with Glory and some of Winston's friends. They planned to work as fast as possible to empty the traps. With Michel piloting the boat Winston could finish the day early.

"So, what do you want to do on your last day?" asked Annette. They were having a leisurely breakfast of boiled eggs and molasses donuts.

"How far is it to Lincolnville Beach?" asked Lacey.

"About forty-five minutes. Why? Is there something you want to do up there?"

"I heard there's a great restaurant for lobster up there," said Lacey.

James raised one eyebrow and looked at her. "Haven't you had enough lobster by now?"

Lacey laughed. "Not yet."

"Say," said Annette thoughtfully. "Why don't we drive up to Acadia National Park, see the sights then stop at Lincolnville Beach for dinner on the way home?"

"That sounds fun," said Lacey.

"There are great hiking trails and we could see the view off Cadillac Mountain. You'll need to wear comfortable shoes," said Annette as she started clearing up the breakfast dishes.

The drive up the coast of Maine on Route 1 took them through Camden, Belfast and Ellsworth. The Atlantic coastline was beautiful under the brilliant autumn sunshine. Sailboats with bright white sails floated on the dark blue water and people played and picnicked on the rocky beaches. Leaving such a beautiful area made Lacey sad. But the thought of all the snow and cold weather coming in a few months convinced her that Arkansas was a better place to wait out the winter. Maybe they would visit again next summer.

While Annette drove and Lacey absorbed the coastline, James read the brochure Annette gave him about Acadia Park.

"Hey listen to this," he said to Lacey. "Cadillac Mountain is located on Mount Desert Island with an elevation of 1,530 feet. Its summit is the highest point of the Atlantic shoreline in the United States. It's known as the first place in the U.S. to see the sunrise."

"I bet the view is fantastic from up there," said Lacey.

It was eleven o'clock when they finally reached the island. Crossing onto the island they took Route 3 toward the park. Tall evergreens lined the road and the smell of pinesap blew in the open car windows. At one point they a saw a moose standing under the trees in the shade.

"My word," said Lacey. "I had no idea a moose was so huge. That one's much bigger than a horse."

HTMLDirect "They'll total a car if you hit one," said Annette. "Every year someone gets killed when they hit a moose. Moose legs are so long the body falls through the windshield."

"Yikes!" said Lacey.

They drove south to the parking area below Cadillac Mountain and parked the car. After the long drive they took a few minutes to stretch their muscles before hiking to the top.

The view was fantastic. The rocky coastline boasted huge boulders interspersed with bushes and wild flowers. The salty air from the water blew up across summit bringing the faint sounds of the seagulls flying over the water. The trees and bushes below were beginning to change into their autumn foliage to yellow, orange and bright red.

"It's so beautiful. What are those islands out there?" asked Lacey pointing to the horizon.

"According to the brochure those are the Porcupine Islands," said James. "Formed by volcanoes and glaciers millions of years ago."

Lacey took photos with her phone and they walked around the top for twenty minutes enjoying the beautiful scenery. By the time they hiked back to the car they were ready for lunch. They drove back to Bar Harbor and found a small restaurant that offered thick cut French fries and the local favorite Wasses hot dogs. Of course Lacey had a lobster roll instead.

Lacey decided to visit some of the local shops and James was soon loaded down with her purchases. "Lace, I don't think you can fit all this stuff in your suitcase," he complained.

"Oh, I know. I'll get a box and mail some of it home," she said smiling.

By the time they returned to Lincolnville Beach for dinner they were exhausted, but Lacey refused to give up this one last chance to eat lobster. They actually ended up with what Mainers' called the Maine Clam Bake. Besides clams, the big steam pot included lobsters, potatoes and corn on the cob with the ever-present melted butter. Even Lacey was satisfied after dinner.

"I think I've finally eaten enough lobster," she said groaning.

James laughed. "At least until next year," he teased.

"Does this mean we can visit next year?" she asked hopefully.

"Yes, it does."

####

The BBQ that evening was being held on the private beach behind Brent West's apartment complex. A fire was already blazing in a pit when Winston and Michel arrived. The smell of grilling burgers floated to them on the salty ocean breeze as they walked across the pebbles down to the beach.

Glory rushed over to greet them. "Hi, Michel. You're looking pretty good for a guy who got kidnapped and almost thrown overboard," she said giving him a hug.

Michel took the opportunity to hug her back. "I'm fine. It's good to see you again."

Glory stepped back and smiled at Winston. Then she got on her tiptoes and kissed his cheek. "Glad you could make it."

A brunette standing by the picnic table called to Glory to help set up the food. "I'll be back," she promised turning to leave.

Winston watched her walk away and felt a wave of happiness wash over him. He couldn't believe someone as talented, brilliant and beautiful as Glory could enjoy his company. He admired the way the tight pants she wore hugged the curve of her hips as she walked.

Brent came up beside Winston and punched him in the arm.

"Ouch! What was that for?" asked Winston looking up at Brent.

"That's just a very small sample of what you'll get if you break Glory's heart," warned Brent. His dark skin glowed in the light of the fire emphasizing the whites of his eyes. "Just thought I'd give you fair warning."

Winston's face grew serious. "I'd never in a million years do anything on purpose that would hurt Glory. Solemn promise," he said.

"What do you mean 'on purpose'?" growled Brent.

"Well, I'm just a guy and often clueless about women so I could screw up."

"Huh, I'll have to let you have a pass on that. We men are clueless sometimes when it comes to the fairer sex," he said before walking away.

Winston introduced Michel to some of the other people standing around the fire pit. After a few minutes Glory called everyone over to the picnic table for dinner. As they lined up to load paper plates with burgers, potato salad and veggies, David Pearson joined the group.

"Hey Winston," said David. "I'd like you to meet my fiancée, Courtney French." The cute blond hanging on his arm smiled at Winston. "Hi," she said shyly.

Winston extended his hand and shook Courtney's hand. "Pleased to meet you."

Courtney brushed a blond lock behind her ear. "David's been telling me about some of your adventures this summer. I want to hear the whole story," she said.

Winston grinned. "I don't think you'd believe half of it." He turned to Michel. "This is my cousin, Michel, he's the one who got kidnapped and almost murdered by drug dealers."

Suddenly all the chatter around the table stopped and everyone looked at Michel whose face turned several shades of red.

"Ok folks, that's the entertainment for the night," said a pretty redhead slipping her hand through Michel's arm. "We want to hear the whole story."

## Chapter 37

"Thank you for coming, Mr. Woods," said DEA Officer Brock Hamilton. "Sorry to pull you in on a Saturday, but I heard this was your last day in Maine and I happened to be in the area. Figured this was the only time I would be able to take your statement myself."

"No problem," said Michel.

"If you'll follow me this way, the Rockland police department has been gracious enough to give the DEA a back room to use for our investigations' team," said Brock. "We've pretty much finished assessing the evidence in this area, but it will be nice to have your statement to round it out."

Michel followed him to a room at the end of the hall that held a table with four chairs, a desk with a computer and other technical equipment.

"Please have a seat. I'll record your statement and after it's typed up I'll need you to read it over and sign it," said Brock. "We have statements from everyone else at the scene the day you were kidnapped, but there's a gap I'd like to fill in." He turned on the recorder. "Saturday, September sixth at nine thirty AM, twenty-twenty-one, this statement is from Michel Woods."

Michel started with the dive that day and what happened on the boat. "Somehow they got the idea that we were spying on them. The older man kept asking me who hired us?"

"That man was William Furman."

Michel nodded. "I heard the other man call him Will."

Brock nodded, "That's pretty much the same statement we have from the others there that day. Then what happened when you were taken?"

Michel explained as much as he could remember from the boathouse. "I was unconscious part of the time, but that's what I remember. After Furman kicked me in the head, I ended up with a concussion."

"How did you get that injury to your hand?"

Michel held up his had with the splinted fingers. "I tried to cut the rope with a piece of broken glass. When I got caught, Will stomped on my hand and broke two fingers."

Brock nodded. That was what Parker Thomas already told them.

"Do you have any idea what they planned to do with you?" asked Brock.

Michel nodded. "From what I heard before they knocked me out I guess they planned to throw me into the ocean."

Brock nodded. "Yes, they did. So this whole thing started because you were diving off Damariscove Island and they thought you, Winston Prescott and Officer Glory Dayes were spying on their drug deals?"

"That's what I gathered from some of the questions they asked. Why would they assume that?" asked Michel.

"I'm not supposed to comment about an ongoing investigation," said Brock. He reached over and stopped the recorder. "I shouldn't tell you this, but William Furman was using that island as a meeting point for deliveries of cocaine first from Canada and lately from New York. When he suspected Richard Prescott of spying, he shot him. We matched the bullet the coroner found in Prescott's body to a gun at Furman's house."

Michel's eyes widened. "Wow. Glad you caught him."

Brock turned the recorder back on. "Thank you for coming in. This interview ended at ten forty-three." He turned off the recorder. "I'll get this typed up." He stood up and shook Michel's hand. "Thank you for coming in." He left Michel sitting in the room.

After a few minutes Glory opened the door. "Hey, Michel. Winston told me you were here to give your statement." She sat down at the table.

He grinned. "Yeah, I guess Officer Hamilton wanted to fill in a few gaps."

She nodded. "We had no idea the DEA was in the area investigating William Furman. I guess it's lucky for us they were here to help. So you're heading home?"

"Tomorrow morning, early. We'll head down to Portland to stay overnight."

"Well, I hope your hand heals quickly. Winston will miss your help," she said.

Michel nodded. "I plan to come back next summer to work on his boat."

"That's great. It's been mostly fun diving with you two," she said before standing up to leave. The door opened and Officer Hamilton came in with papers in his hands.

Michel watched her leave and thought Winston was pretty darn lucky to have her for a girlfriend. He read through the papers and signed the bottom.

Brock led him back to the front where he met Winston.

####

"Hey, Officer Adams," called a male voice.

Devon Adams and Glory turned around to see who it was. They were on lunch break with instructions to bring pizza back to the station.

A skinny blond man walked toward them, a big smile on his face. He wore faded blue jeans and a red shirt.

Devon's face lit up. "Mickey Stearns? Is that you?" He reached out and hugged the man. "Man, you're looking better than I've seen you in years. How are you doing?"

Mickey glanced at the ground shyly. "I'm off the stuff," he said. He looked up at Devon. "After those suppliers got busted I didn't know what to do. I sure didn't want to get on something else, so I checked myself into rehab."

Devon patted him on the shoulder. "I'm happy for you, Mickey. I know you've had it rough. We were worried about you when you disappeared."

"Probably thought you'd find me dead in a ditch somewhere," said Mickey. "I know you tried to help me last year and it didn't take. But this time I'm determined to stay clean."

"Good for you!"

"I've even got a job," he said gesturing to the Speedy Lube logo on his shirt.

Devon grinned. "Hey, that's where I take my car. Guess I'll see you there."

"Yeah, anyway, I just wanted you to know I'm OK," said Mickey. "You and Officer West were the only ones who ever tried to help me."

"Well, I'll let Brent know where to find you. Glad to see you looking so well."

Mickey nodded to Glory and walked away.

Glory looked at Devon with raised eyebrows.

"Mickey was one of our informers. In fact he told us about the cocaine coming in from New York. He's been pretty messed up for a couple of years since his girlfriend died in a fire on his boat," explained. Devon. "I'm happy for him. He was so messed up I figured he'd end up like Belinda and Tommy."

"Those two addicts who were poisoned?" she shuddered.

"Yes. Mickey was probably next on Furman's list."

Glory watched Mickey as he crossed the street. "Guess I'll start going to Speedy Lube."

Devon laughed. "Yeah, they do wicked good work."

## Epilogue

"Mr. Prescott?" said a male voice when Winston answered his phone.

"Yes?"

"This is Albert Manning. I have some very good news for you."

"Great, so the coin sold for a good price?" asked Winston.

Manning chuckled. "Yes, sir, it did. Even after the auction house deducts its fees you'll be receiving a check for almost twenty-five thousand dollars."

Winston gasped. "Really. I never expected to get that much for it."

"Seems there were three collectors bidding for it. You certainly benefit from their bidding war," he said. "I got word from the auction house this morning."

"And no one knows where the coin came from?"

"Absolutely not. I made certain of that."

"Thanks for handling it. I wouldn't have any idea how to go about selling the coin."

"You're certainly welcome," said Manning. "It was my pleasure after getting to see such a rare coin. If you happen to find anything else of value, I'd be happy to help you again."

Winston laughed. "I'll be sure and let you know, but don't hold your breath."

Manning chuckled again. "Best of luck, Mr. Prescott. Good-bye."

"Bye to you, sir."

Annette looked at Winston. "Well, How much did you get?" she asked excitedly.

"He said almost twenty-five thousand dollars after fees," he said smiling.

"Goodness. That's wonderful. That will help with college."

Winston nodded. "I plan to split the money with Michel. After what he went through and all the help he gave me this summer, I won't feel right if I didn't share with him."

Annette hugged him. "I think that's a wonderful idea."

####

"Aw, Winston you don't have to do that," said Michel when Winston called to give him the news about the coin and how he wanted to split the money.

"I know, but you can use it for college, too. It's the right thing to do after all you went through."

"Wow, I don't know how to thank you."

"Just come back next summer and work pulling traps," said Winston.

"I'm already planning to. Thanks again. Talk to you later." Michel sat in silence for several minutes before Lacey finally prodded him.

"What was that about?" she asked as she scooped scrambled eggs onto Michel's plate.

"Winston is getting almost twenty-five thousand dollars for the coin he sold and he's going to split the money with me. I can't believe it," he said.

"What a generous thing to do," said James. His phone rang as he started to take his first bite of toast. He sighed and stood up from the table. "It's Mack," he told Lacey as he walked away.

"Sorry to bother you so early in the morning," apologized Mack. "But I need help with a retrieval. A young girl has gone missing…"

THE END

Made in the USA
Columbia, SC
17 February 2021